"Drop dead, Connor!"

Fern's body was tense with restraint as she continued hotly, "You think you know it all, but you don't. Besides, the long and the short of it is that I'm not answerable to you!"

Connor clicked his tongue disapprovingly, and in a taunting voice asked, "Frustration making you snappy?" The cold cynicism lacing his tone brought goose bumps to her flesh in spite of the warm night. He took a step nearer, saying in suddenly silken tones, "Perhaps I can help."

"Oh, please!" she responded sarcastically. "You're forgetting one thing, Connor. You already said that I wasn't your type—and you certainly aren't mine! I wouldn't get involved with you if you came gift-wrapped in silver ribbons!"

Elizabeth Power was once a legal secretary, but when the compulsion to write became too strong, she abandoned affidavits, wills and conveyances in favor of a literary career. Her husband, she says, is her best critic. And he's a good cook, too—often readily taking over the preparation of meals when her writing is in full flow. They live in a three-hundred-year-old English cottage, surrounded by woodlands and wildlife. Her interests include organic vegetable gardening, regular exercise and ministering to the demands of her generously proportioned cat.

Books by Elizabeth Power

HARLEQUIN ROMANCE
2825—RUDE AWAKENING

HARLEQUIN PRESENTS
1078—SHADOW IN THE SUN
1341—THE DEVIL'S EDEN

Don't miss any of our special offers. Write to us at the following address for information on our newest releases.

Harlequin Reader Service
P.O. Box 1397, Buffalo, NY 14240
Canadian address: P.O. Box 603,
Fort Erie, Ont. L2A 5X3

HOST OF RICHES
Elizabeth Power

Harlequin Books

TORONTO • NEW YORK • LONDON
AMSTERDAM • PARIS • SYDNEY • HAMBURG
STOCKHOLM • ATHENS • TOKYO • MILAN
MADRID • WARSAW • BUDAPEST • AUCKLAND

To Alan—with memories of Paradise

ISBN 0-373-17164-1

HOST OF RICHES

Copyright © 1993 by Elizabeth Power.

This edition published by arrangement with Harlequin Enterprises B. V.

® and TM are trademarks of the publisher. Trademarks indicated with
® are registered in the United States Patent and Trademark Office, the
Canadian Trade Marks Office and in other countries.

Printed in U.S.A.

CHAPTER ONE

SHE woke with a start. Someone was in the flat! She could hear them prowling around outside the bedroom door.

Through a wave of stabbing nausea, Fern tried to switch on the bedside lamp, but couldn't find it. Then she remembered. This was Greg's apartment, or rather his friend's, which he used when he came to London, but he had stormed out earlier tonight—or was it last night now?—when she'd rejected his proposition, and she had crawled in here after he'd gone to lie down because her migraine had been so bad. Had he returned?

The thought sent her blood pumping fearfully through her as the door burst open, intensifying the pain in her already throbbing head, and she shut her eyes tight against the blinding light of the centre beam that was suddenly, mercilessly, thrown on. 'Greg?'

'What the...?' Shock tinged a deep, unfamiliar voice, and, with a shielding hand over her eyes, Fern blinked through the agonising brightness to the dark, masculine figure who appeared momentarily transfixed, still clutching the doorknob, his frame seeming almost to fill the aperture.

'Who the hell are you?' It hurt to speak, like it hurt to move, her own shock overriding fear as the man strode in now, her hazy brain and tortured sight only capable of distinguishing a figure of impressive stature, a dark, dominating figure—dark in every way, from his clothes and his hair to his mood.

5

'I'm sorry to disappoint you, sweetheart, but I'm not Greg. And anyway, I could be asking the same thing about you.' There was authority as well as censure in that voice as he flung open the door of the wardrobe. 'I don't know where your boyfriend's gone—probably back to his wife—but I'm afraid the fun's over now, little girl, because the sole proprietor's back!' Fern winced from the blunt reminder of Greg's marital status that she'd learnt about herself only the previous night. And clearly, because of it, this man thought she was some loose little teenager, doubly misled by her girlish heart-shaped face and that small snub nose that she hated, she realised, as he went on, 'I'm jet-lagged. I'm weary. And after I take a shower I want full occupancy of my own apartment—complete with one double bed— so I'm afraid you're going to have to vacate.'

Eyes barely adjusting, her hair a dishevelled pale cloud across the pillows, hazily Fern recognised the force-fulness behind what she could see now was a strikingly strong-boned profile—the impatience in the hard cast of the prominent, unshaven jaw. He was tugging off the dark shirt, and Fern swallowed nervously, dragging her gaze from an impression of bronzed, muscular flesh and lifting it painfully to his. 'You own this place?'

As she tried to sit up, the nausea overcame her. She was going to be ill! All over his duvet! she thought frantically, somehow managing to scramble out of bed and only making it through to the adjoining bathroom in time.

'Well, well. You really had a good time, didn't you?' As the sickness subsided she heard his deprecating voice coming from the doorway. 'Tell me something—was it the contents of my cocktail cabinet the two of you availed yourself of as well as my bed?'

So he thought she was ill through drink!

Livid, Fern wanted to fling back just how wrong he was, but she was starting to shiver now, her teeth chattering, so that she couldn't say anything. Despairingly, though, she realised how incriminating her clothes—or rather, lack of them—were, her pink satin camisole and french knickers all she was wearing, as she'd pulled off her cotton suit so as not to crease it when, sick and feverish, she'd crept under the duvet earlier, knowing she'd be incapable of getting up again tonight. And here was this…brute insisting she leave the apartment by the time he'd taken a shower! Crouched beside the basin, she dropped her head hopelessly into her hands and groaned.

She heard him curse softly just behind her. Then something was being placed around her shoulders—the red towelling robe she'd seen him take from the wardrobe—and she had no strength to resist the hands that clamped on to her upper arms and drew her to her feet.

'What a state to get into!' His tone was no less censuring for all his sudden display of cool regard. But, ill as she felt, she wasn't oblivious to the latent strength in the arm that lay across her shoulders, to the lingering traces of cologne that clung to his bare chest or how he towered over her five feet six inches as he guided her back to the bedroom. 'I suggest you sleep it off.' It was more of an order than a recommendation, his hand freeing the long honey-blonde hair caught inside the robe so that it fell against the dark fabric in wild disarray. 'You're going to have one hell of a head in the morning, young lady—but, even so, you're going home—wherever that is—first thing. Is that understood?'

'Perfectly.' She flopped down on to the bed, hating to have to accept his hospitality, feeling his hard fingers over hers as she tried to pull off his robe.

'Keep it. You could well need it more than I do,' he stated drily, and she sensed rather than saw his disparaging grimace. Which meant that he fully expected her to be up half the night with alcoholic poisoning! she decided through her debilitated senses, when she had had nothing other than one glass of wine with her dinner hours before. But she felt too sick to begin to explain, too weak even to curse Greg for bringing her here in the first place.

'You were su-supposed to be away,' she commented feebly, watching him move back to the wardrobe, conscious, even in her sick state, of the perfect musculature of his broad, bare back, of the way he moved, despite his build and height, with such lean almost athletic grace. Hadn't Greg said he always used this place in favour of a hotel when he was in town? An arrangement he'd come to with the owner whenever he was away. Through blurred reasoning she seemed to recall Greg saying that his friend was abroad on business. 'Would you have turned me out as quickly if I'd been Greg—your friend,' she summoned up the strength to challenge emphatically, 'or is anybody in residence only given a moment's notice when the landlord comes back and decides he wants his bed?'

There was a tough implacability in the stranger's face as he turned to look at her, shrugging into a soft-looking casual shirt.

'The arrangement was that this place would be for your boyfriend's sole inhabitance—not for the conducting of extra-marital relations with any little harlot who just happens to take his fancy.'

'Little har...!' If she had felt better, Fern thought, she would have hit him. As it was, just the adrenalin her anger produced was enough to bring the waves of sickness washing over her again so that she was forced to take his verbal abuse, relieved when he muttered curtly, 'Get some sleep,' and, striding back across the room, snapped off the light, the door he closed behind him enclosing her in a dark cocoon of silence.

Shivering, Fern pulled the robe more closely around her and slipped down under the quilt. She felt so sick and cold. Miserably her thoughts wandered back through the nauseous fog of her migraine to the man who she'd thought was her friend until tonight, when she'd realised what his only interest in her was. It was Greg Peters who had told her about the vacancy with the advertising agency six months ago, a firm he had had close association with through his own involvement with the advertising world. She was a graphic designer with a small firm, and her prospects had looked very bleak, but the job with a bigger company had not only allowed her to exploit and develop her artistic talents, but had also led to her new position of art director when the firm had been taken over by Harrison Stone, a massive international agency, only last week. And all because of Greg, she'd thought fondly until tonight. She hadn't seen him that often, as he lived and worked primarily in York, and, as he held a similar post with another agency, their involvement had always been on a business footing, until he had invited her out socially a month ago.

It had been an enjoyable evening—like others that had followed—his light parting kiss on her cheek when he'd left her at night assuring her he had had no intention of rushing her into a serious relationship—and for which she had respected him, finding him refreshingly different from most of the other men she had known who expected her to jump into bed with them after the first kiss, and then lost interest in her when she showed total disinclination to comply. Greg wasn't like that—or so she'd thought, she reflected with a mental grimace that only gave strength to the merciless hammering inside her head. When he had taken her to dinner last night, she'd realised she was beginning to look on him as more than a friend—as someone who could possibly become special to her—his apparent appreciation of her mind instead of just her body, shown by his eagerness to share his thoughts, invite her opinions and advice over his work— like those new cover designs he'd been working on— only increasing her respect for him, so that she didn't see any need to flinch from his request afterwards for her supposedly valued thoughts on the designs he had taken to the apartment to work on. She would have refused, already recognising the dreaded symptoms of an incipient migraine, but he'd seemed so genuinely desperate for a second opinion that she hadn't had the heart to.

It was only then that she had discovered he'd had other designs besides those he kept so neatly in his loose-leaf binder! Oh, he'd secured her advice on those all right— before he'd shed the lambswool he'd been pulling so cleverly down over her eyes and turned into a ravaging, sex-crazed wolf!

She had responded to his persuasive kisses at first, but tentatively, aware as she had been of the intimacy of the place, and not wanting their relationship to take off before she had barely accepted that it was on the move. And then he'd told her the truth—very plainly and very startlingly—that he was married, but that they could use this apartment whenever they could get it if she was willing to see him on that basis.

If she could have gone then, she would have, but she was without her car, since Greg had picked her up from her own flat. So instead she had stood there, her temper flaring, her disappointment, dismay and anger at his deceit, his outrageous audacity, precipitating the blinding headache that had held her prisoner in this apartment, her anger somehow igniting his passion so that she had had to fight off his unwelcome advances, her only salvation being when she had pulled away from him and doubled up against the back of the sofa into which she had stumbled, groaning from her very real sickness, so that, mercifully, he'd taken it as a slight against himself, and slammed out of the flat. Fern had been too ill to do anything then but drag herself into the bedroom, where she must have fallen asleep before that hunk of condemnation burst in...

A dull grey light coming through the open curtains presaged another chilly June day. Frowning, feeling uncomfortably hot, Fern blinked herself fully awake, the sight of a man's shirt discarded over a chair and the few personal masculine effects on the chest of drawers that matched the quality wood of the wardrobe bringing it all back to her. Greg, and the tall, condemning stranger who had helped her even while his tongue had flayed.

She groaned, realising she felt so sticky because she was still wearing his robe and, craving a shower, she carefully got out of bed.

Fortunately her migraine was gone, leaving her feeling excessively fragile with the usual tenderness above one eye. The shower refreshed her, though, making her feel somewhat better as she reached for one of the large clean fluffy towels which, surprisingly, he had left on the edge of the bath for her, because the one he had used was drying on the rail against the tiled wall, and she couldn't remember the others being there last night.

The smell of bacon cooking wafted towards her as she came into the lounge, cool in her sleeveless floral-patterned blouse and matching calf-length culottes. The large, modern room with its classic furniture and pale striped walls looked considerably more inviting this morning after last night's ordeal there with Greg, the open flight-bag and books, keys and a few odd coins lying on the coffee-table adding to an ambience that had already looked comfortably lived-in. Even so, Fern flinched from the memory, a memento of pain throbbing sickeningly across her temple.

'Good morning.' The man was turning the sizzling bacon in the pan on the stove, the sidelong glance he'd given her as she appeared in the doorway a wry appraisal of the wild blonde hair framing the pale heart of her face, of the dark half-moons she was too aware of beneath the pained hazel of her eyes. 'Do you want some breakfast?'

It smelt good, but her stomach rebelled, so she decided it was best not to risk it.

'No, thanks. Just some of that coffee.' She jerked her chin towards the pot of dark liquid on the kitchen counter, wincing as her temple throbbed again.

'Sit down.' There was sagacity in the deep-voiced command which compelled her to obey, and from a seat at the pine table she made a casual observation of his kitchen. It was like the rest of the place—large, but with none of the ostentation she might have expected of a place in a top-rate suburb like this. Just entirely functional, totally male-orientated and thoroughly lived in. 'You look awful,' he added.

'Thanks,' she riposted, feeling the sting in his remark, sensing that hard disapproval of the early hours returning in force, and a pained furrow appeared between her eyes. 'You don't exactly look like the prize catch of London yourself.'

Unshaven still, in light faded jeans, with a white T-shirt hugging his powerful torso, he had a black smudge of what looked like oil on the hard tan of his cheek. There was something wholly animal about him, though, a primeval male attraction that disquieted her, Fern was reluctant to acknowledge as, ignoring her retaliatory remark, he flicked a switch on the wall before turning out the bacon on to a plate and cracking two eggs into the frying-pan.

Watching him drop a tea-bag into a cup and scald it with the boiling water from the kettle, absently Fern wondered what he did for a living.

'Here.' She frowned as he set the cup and saucer down in front of her, looking up into his face.

It was a strong, well-determined face, etched with character. A high forehead, intense brown eyes beneath heavy lids, and what she could easily have termed a passionate—yet somehow cruel—mouth, emphasised by the devil-dark stubble that clung to that forceful jaw. He had to be several years older than Greg, she calculated, from the fine lines at the corners of those penetrating eyes and the hard-hewn grooves beneath those prominent cheekbones, putting him at around thirty-four or five. But that very maturity gave him an aura of such vital sexuality that she dropped her gaze to her steaming cup, feeling oddly discomposed.

'Drink it,' he ordered. 'It'll do you some good. Contrary to public belief, tea's far more beneficial for a hangover than coffee.'

'You'd know, of course,' she uttered, piqued because he was still assuming—had instantly assumed—that she had had too much to drink last night without even bothering to ask her if anything else might be wrong. But when he chose to ignore that too, she merely mumbled thanks, and sipped gratefully at the tea.

'What's your name?' He was lifting out the eggs, not even glancing her way, as though she wasn't even worth a second look.

Putting her cup down into her saucer with a small, hollow sound, Fern answered with a sugary sweetness, 'Are you really that interested?'

This time her sarcasm had its effect, because, dumping the plate and his cup and saucer down on the table opposite her, he sat down, saying with a cold implacability, 'Only in so far as I prefer not to eat breakfast with a total stranger. But if you're imagining you can flash those pretty eyelashes at me with the same result you got from Greg, forget it, sweetheart. You just aren't my type.'

Fern's nostrils flared. 'And what makes you think you're mine?' she snapped back, flabbergasted by the outrageous conceit of the man as he began calmly slicing through his bacon, the aroma of his strong black coffee drifting towards her. All this antagonism, though, wasn't doing her head any good at all, and sufferingly she dropped it forward on to her splayed hands, supported by her elbows on the table.

Opposite, she heard her host's chair creak, sensed that he was sitting back to look at her. 'Just how much did the two of you have last night?' he demanded.

Fern peered out from under her hands, smarting from the censure in his voice. There he was, doing it again— totally prejudging her.

She lifted a deliberately careless shoulder. If he'd summed her up as a drunken little tramp the instant he'd walked through the door then that was his problem. He could go on thinking what he liked! She might have told him the truth last night if she had been well enough to explain. But as it was, he'd immediately jumped to all the wrong conclusions, and right now she was feeling too anti-men—all men!—to have to start defending her actions in front of a total stranger—and a pompous, overbearing one at that!

'Do you have a name?' He sat forward, slicing into the perfectly cooked egg, clearly not allowing any-thing—even her—to upset his appetite, or his routine. He was probably the type who did everything perfectly too, she thought, glancing resentfully around the prac-tical, well-fitted modern kitchen.

This time she told him, picking up her cup again, the red-tipped fingers of the hand thrust into her hair a stark contrast against the pale strands. 'So what about you? Do you have one? Or do they just call you "sir"?'

A thick eyebrow climbed upwards, and his lips compressed wryly at her carefully aimed snipe. But, sounding totally unperturbed, he answered, 'Connor McManus.'

Connor McManus. Fern considered it for a moment. It suited him down to the ground—hard, imposing and raw-edged as flint.

'Irish?' It came out as a sneer, which he ignored, picking up a thick chunk of wholemeal bread from a plate in the centre of the table.

'Not for three generations.'

'And I take it there can't possibly be a Mrs McManus?'

That was a gibe too, deliberately implying how insufferable she imagined he'd be to live with, and she paid for it when he dropped his knife and fork and sat back to fix her with a glare of chilling contempt which didn't even compare with the glacial quality in his voice as he tossed back, 'Why? Would it make me more interesting to you if there were?'

It was such a shearing remark—carefully chosen to cut her down to size—that for a moment she was lost for a suitable response, feeling angry, embarrassed colour stealing across her skin.

'Well, now we've got that over with, Fern Baxter, perhaps you could throw some light on those banknotes carelessly abandoned over my settee. Are they yours?'

He was referring to the money Greg had thrown down for her transport home before he'd walked out in a huff—money she wouldn't have used even if she had been well enough to leave—and she couldn't keep the acidity out of her voice as she answered, 'No, they're your precious friend Greg's—and you can keep them!'

'Oh, I see.' His mouth quirked in shrewd acknowledgement. 'Now I think I'm beginning to get the picture.'

He picked up his knife and fork again, finishing the last mouthful. 'What was it, Fern? A lovers' quarrel?' When she didn't answer, not wishing to remember last night, let alone discuss it with this arrogant stranger, he was enquiring, 'How long have you known him?'

Fern shrugged, a delicate movement beneath the red floral blouse. 'Longer than I should have,' she told him truthfully, swallowing some more of her tea.

She felt the penetrating intensity of those brown eyes upon her, assessing, appraising, as he put down his knife and fork. 'Let me guess.' The wooden chair protested again as he leaned back against it. 'You've acted the part of the dutiful mistress so far as he's wanted, and now you want him to divorce his wife, but he won't play ball.'

He was so far off the mark that she almost wanted to laugh, except that this whole situation was far from funny. She'd been both hurt and disgusted by Greg's behaviour, as she'd always kept as far away from married men as she could possibly get, having too much respect for the close-knit union of two people; a thing instilled in her by her parents, whose own marriage had always been happy. And here was this supercilious Connor McManus having tried, judged and sentenced her without an inkling of what she was really like or the firm code of ethics by which she lived.

The thought rankled, and anger lit her eyes as she finished the dregs of the surprisingly refreshing tea and stood up.

'Is it experience, or just sheer brilliance that makes you so clever?' she enquired pointedly, although her throat contracted when she saw the glitter of anger beneath the heavy eyelids that made his eyes shine like chips of coal.

'You don't give a damn, do you, how his wife stands in all this?' The quiet vehemence with which he spoke had a quivering effect on her nerves. She ignored the accusation, however, and went over to the bright copper sink to rinse the crockery she had just used, staring abstractedly out on to a rather unkempt garden.

A patio, bearing the remains of a recent barbecue, gave on to lawn, well overdue for a trim, and there was a bright yellow ball peeping, abandoned, out of the long grass. Probably it had come over from a neighbouring garden, she surmised with some astringency now. And which he'd probably been too mean to throw back! 'As a matter of interest, what do your parents think about your behaviour?' His chair scraped the floor as he got up. 'Or don't they know anything about it?' he quizzed, contempt in every imposing inch of him as she left the crockery to drain and turned back to face him again, swallowing hard. He was too close, the threatening proximity of him invading her personal space, making her feel strangely ill at ease.

'Why?' she enquired, wishing she had taken up her parents' offer to spend a week with them in their new Lakeland home, far from London and all the problems she was facing at the moment. 'Are you going to make it your business to tell them, Connor?' she invited sweetly in mock challenge, deciding that, if he'd labelled her a harlot without waiting to hear her side of things first, then he really wasn't worth the trouble of putting straight.

'No,' he said, surveying her with a hard, cynical watchfulness while she dried her hands on a towel. 'But if I were your father I'd lay my hand so hard across your pretty backside you wouldn't even blink at another married man again. How old are you? Eighteen? Nineteen?'

'I'm twenty-four!' She read the shock in his eyes from her indignant riposte, exasperated with her youthful looks that had had him making the same mistake as everyone else. Even so, an oddly panicking note had crept into her voice from a disturbing inner tension, brought on by a shattering awareness of his compelling masculinity and the mortifying picture of being physically subdued by him. It made her feel sick. Or was it her head? She didn't know any more.

'Strange though it may seem, I've managed to run my life up until now more than adequately without any assistance from you!' she snapped, sensing the threatening anger emanating from him with his body heat as she brushed past him, wanting to get out of his way—out of his flat! 'I've had about as much of your moralising as I can possibly take. Thanks for the hospitality! I'm going home.'

She was almost in the lounge when she felt the painful strength of his fingers on her arm just below her sleeve, terminating her attempt at a dignified retreat.

'On foot?'

Obviously those kestrel-keen eyes must have noted the lack of any strange vehicle outside. There was cold mockery, though, in every tough line of his face, so that, with an unwise toss of her head which caused it to throb with cruel anguish, she spat, 'If I have to!'

'Don't be so silly.' He had caught both arms now and turned her to face him, hard eyes digesting the bloodless pallor of her skin. 'You aren't in any fit state—any fool can see that.'

'Why should you care?' His touch, with that dauntingly potent energy she could feel in him, unnerved her, though she wasn't usually one to be easily intimidated, and as the pressure of his hands relaxed she pulled herself free. 'You've already assessed what I'm like so perfectly with your accurate, high-minded brain. So why not just throw me out on the street? I would have thought that would have given you immense delight. My "come-uppance", don't you think?'

His eyes narrowed contemptuously above the fierce black shadow of jaw-stubble, and he slipped his hands into his pockets, causing the dark denim to pull tightly across his hips.

'You really don't have one iota of conscience, do you?' he rasped, his features dark and despising as he stood there regarding the slender lines of her body beneath the thin floral suit. 'Doesn't it trouble you that he has a wife—and one who's expecting his baby? Or doesn't a girl like you care one way or the other whether the child grows up without a father just because she wants something that doesn't belong to her, regardless of the cost?'

A *baby*? Fern stood, inwardly shaken, wondering if her shock showed. Greg hadn't said anything about a baby when he'd confessed to being married last night, she realised, wondering why he'd even bothered to do that. Disgust sickening her, she swayed, grabbing the door-jamb, her head lifting in a way that could have been mistaken for rebellion, instead of a desperate determination to keep Connor McManus from guessing just how giddy she felt, as, refusing to bend before his totally unjust accusations—though she could appreciate how it must look to him—she met those dark, despising eyes to say in a voice husky with conviction, 'If it hadn't been me, it would probably have been someone else.'

It was the wrong thing to say, and despairingly she realised it when his mouth pulled down so hard that the harshening grooves beneath his cheeks lent him a look of stone. 'You unscrupulous little——' For one terrified moment she thought he was going to strike her, and fear showed unwittingly in her eyes as his seemed to impale her with unrelenting distaste.

She should have explained. Swallowed her pride and told him the truth! she thought hectically, hearing the contraction of the cooling stove—the only sound she was conscious of above the nervous pounding in her ears.

But then, with a harshly drawn breath, he was swinging away from her, towards the spare bedroom, almost as if it were the only way he could stop himself from hurting her, saying with a deadly softness, 'You're right. I think you'd better go home.'

She was in the lounge, gathering her belongings together, when he strode back in, a denim jacket thrown on over the T-shirt.

'You live in London, I take it?'

When she didn't answer, not wanting even to give him the satisfaction of a reply, he said, 'Are you ready?'

From the sudden jangling of his keys it was startlingly evident that he intended to drive her himself.

'That isn't necessary,' Fern said tensely, stuffing a comb into her bag. 'I can call a cab.'

'Maybe—but you aren't going to. Who knows what time it might get here? And I was rather looking forward to sharing the rest of the weekend with some enjoyable companionship, something rather more principled—so, if you don't mind, I'd prefer to see you well and truly off the premises before she arrives.'

Which told her! Fern thought, bristling, deciding from the way he'd just relegated his girlfriend to a 'something' that he was patently a total sexist as well!

'Why not disinfect the place too, so she doesn't catch anything?' she retorted scathingly as he opened the door for her to precede him out of the apartment, but he refused to respond this time, silently escorting her across the sandy-gravelled area to his car. A humble saloon that had certainly seen better days, she decided, and, casting a furtive glance at his unshaven, laid-back appearance as he started the unhealthy-sounding engine, she wondered how he could afford to live in such an expensive area.

He hadn't said a word to her, except to ask directions, until he pulled up outside the small Victorian house in the more modest suburb where she lived. Now, though, as she was experiencing some difficulty with opening her door, he leaned across to help her, his sudden closeness, with the tang of some soap he'd used and that other, more elusive scent of his skin, so impinging that she pressed herself back against the seat, tension coiling inexplicably inside her. 'I shan't say it's been nice,' he breathed in low, condemnatory tones. 'But then I didn't have the pleasure, did I? However, if you find yourself abandoned in my bed again, perhaps some other time.'

Hard mockery touched the cruel mouth at the angry, embarrassed colour suffusing her cheeks, and then with a casual ease he released the lever, opening her door.

Quickly Fern scrambled out, flinging back over her shoulder through the fine, cold drizzle. 'I wouldn't go to bed with you if you were the last man on earth! Apart from which, you couldn't afford me!' Anger and frustration had her snapping impetuously, discrediting her still further in his eyes. But what did it matter? she thought irately, as she slammed the car door, heard the saloon coughing away. She certainly wouldn't be seeing *him* again!

CHAPTER TWO

'NOT going to get a summer this year, dear—that's what they've forecast.' Queenie was polishing the brass knocker as Fern came down into the hall, one look at the chilly, wet day making her glad she had chosen to wear her long-sleeved red blouse beneath the tailored grey suit. 'When I realised you hadn't come home yesterday morning, I went up and fed the fish. I must say you looked ever so pale when you stepped out of that car, dear. Are you sure you're fit to go to work?'

Seventy, widowed, with one married son who was the apple of her eye, Queenie Smith lived on the ground floor, and, as well as being Fern's landlady, was also a valued neighbour and friend. Which gave her the right to be just a little bit curious about her private life, Fern thought fondly, when, as she assured her that she was, the woman went on disconcertingly to ask, 'A special date, was he? He looked ever so nice.'

Queenie was just being kind, she thought. She knew the men Fern dated usually looked far more conservative—not the type she'd be reluctant to take home for Sunday tea!

'Just a friend of a friend,' she responded loosely with a grimace, and, thanking Queenie for her thoughtfulness, tripped hurriedly down the steps to the sporty Fiesta.

'Looking your professional best today,' the receptionist laughed over the top of her newspaper when Fern arrived at the agency with her usual half an hour to spare, because this morning she had used more make-up to hide the pallor of her skin, securing her hair at the nape of her neck in the hope that the severity of the style would make her look older, more sophisticated; and both because since the takeover last week she hadn't yet met her new boss, the ruling hand at the helm, and he was due in this morning. So it was with a twinge of nerves that she made her way through the warren of Victorian rooms to the second floor, to find that all her preconceived ideas about her new boss were entirely wrong as she came face to face with him in her office.

'Fern Baxter, I believe.' A portly, balding man was moving towards her, the chubby hand taking hers, as warm as his smile, as he said with a hint of north country, 'Franklin Stone. They told me you were my new art director, but at the risk of sounding outrageously sexist, young lady, I wasn't told you were quite so pretty!'

Fern smiled, instantly warming to this avuncular, jovial-looking man, deciding that the future stood to be very pleasant if Franklin Stone was all he seemed.

Naturally, as she expected, it was a hectic morning. The phone didn't stop ringing, and, in between amalgamating files and intermingling new systems and references with the old, Fern was kept busy speaking to clients, model agencies and photographers, immensely relieved that, although she still felt somewhat fragile from her migraine, she was at least able to cope. Fortunately, too, the other unpleasant aspects of her weekend were gradually fading, losing their importance under the enjoyable pressure of her job.

What Greg had wanted her to do was unpardonable, she thought, as she stole a moment to sip the coffee someone had brought her. But what had happened after he'd gone...well, really it was funny when she looked back on it—the way that insufferable brute who had owned the flat had leapt to all those conclusions about her, and how she had let him go on believing them to the very last. He was probably still fumigating the place, she decided with a small relishing smile as she pictured him after he'd left her, shooting back and racing round the apartment with the air freshener to hide all traces of her perfume before his very *principled* ladyfriend arrived.

And how he'd spoken about *her*! As if she was a chattel rather than a person, which just proved what an all-round lowly view he had of women in general, even if he'd thought *she* was the lowest. And that was what made the whole thing so ironic, because, heaven knew, she had faults like anybody else. But promiscuity wasn't one of them. And yet, amusing though it was, a shudder ran the length of her spine when she thought about the way she had acted—the things she had let him believe— realising that if she'd been in his shoes she'd probably have thought exactly the same thing.

It was only the probability that she would never see him again that relegated him to the back of her mind, together with Franklin Stone's invitation to lunch.

'You've heard of Aqua-Leisure International, I take it?' he enquired across the table in the small, oak-beamed Italian restaurant, where the pungent smell of garlic and other gastronomical scents acted tantalisingly on Fern's nostrils.

'ALI?' Fern's hair gleamed gold as she looked up at her employer. 'Is there anyone who knows anything about water sports who hasn't?' she responded, smiling. 'It's only the most successful manufacturer of water-sports equipment in Europe, with a chain of retail outlets throughout the world!' Linked to it were subsidiary companies involved in the manufacture and development of marine craft with an emphasis on speed and sport, she remembered, and, with a father whose passion was boats, she was eternally acquainted with the company's latest developments.

'My last art director—your predecessor,' Franklin Stone clarified, 'was working on their latest brochure. But he didn't like the changes that being part of a larger company meant with this takeover, so he left, smack in the middle of it all—which is why I'm turning the job over to you to finish. Their chief executive is a personal friend of mine, but I can't afford to take any chances. He's my biggest client, and he's got to have the same satisfaction from us as he had before or the whole darn account—and that includes various companies within the ALI group—could be lining some other agency's pockets. I've seen some of your work and I'm very impressed, so it's all down to you to keep ALI from going elsewhere.' He bent down to open his briefcase and handed her a file. 'In there are a few examples of the sort of thing we've done for him before and the type of quality he expects from us. I'm expecting great things from you.'

He was indeed, Fern thought, as she thumbed through it, appreciating the high standard of the previous years' brochures, pleased, yet a little unnerved, by the strength of his agency's faith in her capabilities.

A smart, black-bowed waiter appeared, but Franklin was waving him away, consulting a large gold pocket-watch which he tucked back into his waistcoat. 'Well? Any comments?' he invited.

'Yes. I think——'

'Franklin!' Suddenly another, deeper voice was breaking in. 'You'll have to excuse my being late, but I had to drop Honey off at the college. I think at the end of this term she'll...'

Whatever Honey was hoping to do at college, Fern didn't hear, all her senses paralysed by the deep tones of the man behind her chair, whose face she hadn't yet seen—didn't need to—that voice alone impinging on her ears with shocking recognition. Connor McManus!

'Connor...come and meet my new art director, Fern Baxter. As I told you earlier on the phone, she's damn good! Fern, meet the chief executive of Aqua-Leisure International...'

As her employer got up, making the introductions, Fern's mind raced, what reasoning powers she could summon up assuring her that the chances of this situation arising were about a million to one—that this couldn't be happening! But it was. And as she turned discomfitingly to the man standing beside her now, she had to stifle a gasp. The clean-cut, sophisticated image he presented in a tailored silver-grey suit, white shirt and silver tie was so different from the one he'd sported at that apartment that Fern felt as though she'd been punched in the ribs.

He smiled, a cold, emotionless smile, mocking her obvious shock, and her throat contracted as a strong, warm hand clasped hers in brief formality.

'Fern.' If his handshake had been businesslike, then her name was spoken with such blatant familiarity that panic showed for a moment in her fine features, making her heart pound. Grief, what was he doing here? her mind ran on chaotically, aware of the cruel satisfaction playing around his mouth. Probably from her discomfort! she thought, too embarrassed to look at him, catching a disturbing waft of his aftershave lotion as he sat down on her right between her and her employer, concealing his own surprise with such impeccable reserve that she wondered if Franklin had mentioned her name to him prior to their meeting.

'So you've dropped her at the college, have you?' In a blind daze, Fern heard Franklin commenting to his prestigious client. 'And how is Sabrina Bianca—or Honey, as you prefer to call the lovely lady in your life? Sitting for her finals yet?' His ample middle shook as they shared a joke Fern failed to see. 'I expect she'll leave with honours at the very least.'

'She's counting on it.' It was an absent, almost bored response from Connor, as if he were tired of the subject of his clearly very intellectual girlfriend. As he'd probably tire of the woman—any woman—before long, Fern was surprised to find herself thinking, her eyes resting unwittingly on the wry curve of his mouth that even in her feeble state yesterday she had recognised as cruel. A man who expected the best and who would make apologies to no one, she thought with a little shudder, because it was Franklin, he'd said, who *had* to excuse *him* when he'd been delayed.

'I was about to acquaint Fern with the reason we're here.' The older man sent Connor an almost conspiratorial glance before smiling in her direction. 'Connor and I are old friends, and I've watched him come from nowhere, right from when he was a struggling student who used to help my doting adolescent daughter with her homework, to the big name he is today. Rumour has it he's a multi-millionaire, lass, although he'll probably deny it.' He laughed loudly. 'I only know I'd like some of that hard-hitting energy in my company, but he's too busy manufacturing and retailing to take up with advertising as well.'

'Oh, I don't know.' Disconcertingly, since he had sat down, Connor McManus hadn't taken his eyes off Fern, and uncomfortably now, with her gaze fixed on the silver cutlery on the white damask cloth, she could feel that dark gaze moving with lazy appraisal over the tense planes and contours of her face. 'With an art director like Fern, it might be possible to tempt me. Or I could perhaps seduce her away from you, if I offered her the right kind of contract. Tell me something, Franklin. Is she...expensive?'

His carefully chosen words had Fern's eyes lifting to meet his humourless smile, the cold satisfaction in his eyes. She swallowed, and was glad of the rosy shading on her cheeks that concealed the colour she could feel scorching them, knowing full well that he wasn't referring to her claim on the payroll! Abashed, she was regretting every second she'd spent not bothering to explain herself the previous day—and particularly that parting shot as she'd stepped out of his car. If he was ALI's number-one man he could afford anything, although, ironically, she thought, he'd be the type women would chase—and not just for the things he could afford!

Fortunately then the waiter came back to their table, and the next few minutes were spent making their various choices from the menu.

At Franklin's request, Connor was studying the wine list, and above the hum of conversation around them that rich, resonant voice was suddenly asking, 'Which would you prefer, Fern?' He suggested one or two he thought would best complement the lasagne she had chosen, his sudden personal interest in her preference seeming somehow strangely intimate—like that first use of her name—while the waiter hovered with polished hospitality, waiting for Connor to state their decision.

'If you don't mind, I think I'll just stick with the orange juice,' she asserted to her employer, touching the upturned base of her wine glass in a negating gesture. And for Connor's benefit, 'I seldom drink anything stronger—particularly at lunchtime, Mr McManus.' So swallow that! she thought smugly, and saw those brown eyes narrow in unveiled speculation before he agreed something with Franklin and the waiter disappeared.

'A lady who doesn't drink! Quite a paragon you've got here, Franklin.' Surely only she could detect the cynicism in that deep, sardonic voice? 'Do you believe her?' Clearly he wasn't content to leave it there. She'd been drunk in his bed after an adulterous night with Greg Peters as far as he was concerned, and obviously he wasn't going to let her forget it—not that quickly, she realised, with an apprehensive little shudder.

'Why shouldn't he?' she contested, a reckless defiance in the hazel eyes that belied her polite, jaw-aching smile. Sweat dampened her skin as those brown irises darkened, glittered with an ominous satisfaction that told her he was more than delighted to rise to her challenge.

'Probably because paragons are rare—particularly when they're so... beautifully packaged.' Those heavy lids were lowered as his gaze embraced the slender curvature of her body, his thick, long lashes as black as night against the olive of his skin. Fern tensed, conscious of that hard self-assurance behind the arrogant tilt of his head, of that glaring, untrammelled masculinity, and a flood of hot emotions surged through her. Perhaps most women wouldn't mind being visually stripped by him, but she wasn't one of them! And even if she didn't have to know him to realise how intrepid and commanding some people might find him, it didn't impress her one bit!

Another waiter brought the wine, and after Connor's approval filled two glasses with the dark liquid, and moved discreetly away.

Fern sipped her cool juice and then, with an affected exterior calmness, allowed her gaze to travel with slow, deliberate assessment over the hard cast of Connor's cheek and jaw, down the corded strength of his throat to the wide shoulders beneath the expensive cut of his jacket, and with a forced, demure smile she uttered sweetly, 'Perhaps, Mr McManus, you should never judge others by yourself.'

What on earth had possessed her to say that? For one heart-stopping moment she wondered if she had gone too far. She was supposed to be keeping him happy, after all! But with a loud burst of laughter from the opposite side of the table, Franklin was chuckling, 'Well, well, Connor, you really asked for that!'

Out of the corner of her eye Fern saw Connor's mouth curl in cool acknowledgment, her attention drawn fully towards him now as he lifted his glass in a brief, salutory gesture.

'Perhaps,' he acceded softly, in response to her alone, that mask of smiling urbanity leaving those glittering eyes as chilling as frost. 'But when one knows what's beneath the packaging...'

Fern's glass almost toppled over as she set it down on the crisp white cloth, her hand trembling with shock. He wouldn't...?

One look at the hard resolve in those austere features assured her that he would—and get immense satisfaction out of doing so.

'Do you two know each other?' Franklin was enquiring, frowning as he looked from one to the other.

The clink of cutlery and glasses, and the loud metallic ring as a pan was dropped somewhere in the kitchen, barely registered with her as Connor sent her a blazing smile and said quietly, 'Do we, Fern?'

Numbed into silence, she didn't know what to say. She could feel herself growing hotter under the immaculate grey suit, the red silk of her blouse seeming to stick to her. No amount of blusher, she knew, could hide the riotous colour suffusing her cheeks, but then she heard the man beside her laugh softly before taking a leisurely draught of his wine, the ruby liquid rich and dark against the contrasting brilliance of his shirt cuff. 'Obviously Fern's too prudent to elucidate on our past...acquaintanceship,' mortified, she heard the deep voice conveying.

But the older man, clearly misunderstanding, was exchanging another knowing look with his client, saying, 'I see. Does that mean she knows?'

'Not yet.'

Through an uncomfortable, damp warmth, Fern sensed something ominous, although whatever it was she was supposed to know had to wait, because their entrées arrived, so that it was a few moments before her employer started to explain.

'As I mentioned to you earlier, Fern, we're currently compiling ALI's new brochure with everything from the latest wet-suits to the most advanced diving equipment, to be photographed in the scuba divers' paradise itself— Bermuda. One of that country's treasure-hunters, Ross Walker, has agreed to endorse the new range of ALI's diving products, and Connor's flying out there himself in a week or two to see how things are done. I know you've never done anything on this sort of scale before, but I'm giving you the chance—if you feel you'd like to take it—to fly out with him when he goes, to handle all his company's requirements out there—organise everything, and generally see that Connor's looked after properly on behalf of Harrison Stone. Now I know it's a tall order and a lot to ask of you, and I'll understand if you feel you don't want to take it on. I can easily get someone else only too willing to go, but I'm giving you the choice first, and you'll have a team with you, of course. So what do you say?'

What could she say? *I detest the man? There's no way that I could possibly fly to Bermuda with him?* She saw that cruel mouth twist sardonically at her confusion, and, breath held, she toyed with her dressed avocado slices on the fine bone-china plate, searching desperately for a convincing way out.

'It sounds nice,' she breathed with feigned wistfulness, although it would have been, she thought, if she'd been going with someone—anybody—else! 'I think, though, that, as you said, coming from a smaller company I haven't really had enough experience to handle a venture for a group the size of ALI, and I think it probably would be wise in this instance, for the sake of both companies, if you could send someone else.' After all, as Franklin had said himself, he wouldn't have any difficulty finding someone else to jump into her shoes. And it certainly wouldn't be any great loss to the chief executive of ALI!

Or would it? From the taut set of his jaw she could see that he was angry. That, for some perverse reason known only to himself, he had wanted her to accept.

A gleam of triumph lit the gaze that clashed unwaveringly with his. He was seeing a woman today. One who was in control of her life, who made her own decisions. Not the sick, fragile creature she had been yesterday whom he had mistakenly taken for an adolescent. Maybe she had been thrown off balance seeing him again. Who wouldn't have been? she reasoned. And maybe he had had her on the edge of her seat earlier when he'd seemed bent on exposing those unfortunate yet totally erroneous facts about her to Franklin, but he didn't actually *know* how much he had made her suffer. And if that devastating magnetism of his affected her, then she'd certainly made an impact on him, because ever since he'd arrived he'd scarcely given his attention to anything else. She felt his gaze now, like a tactile thing, tracing the smooth contours of her face; felt its slow, studied interest as it sketched the finely defined brows, the small snub nose and the alluring scarlet of her lips, and, smug in her femininity, she concealed her unease with a smile of such devastating brilliance that she wished she had toned it down a little when, surprisingly, Franklin excused himself to make a phone call and she suddenly found herself alone with Connor.

'So that's that, is it?' he said, and, finishing the course that she had barely started, angled towards her, one arm supported by the back of his chair. The movement exposed a good deal of white shirt, a far too potent reminder of that muscular chest with its dark shading of body hair beneath.

'Don't take it personally,' she purred with an enforced lightness she was certain that clever brain could too easily detect, especially when the firm mouth compressed, his gaze lancing over her with contemplative speculation.

'No?' An eyebrow lifted, derisive and sceptical. 'What, then? Because whether you convinced Stone or not, your claim to inexperience certainly didn't convince me. I know the man well enough to be assured that he doesn't employ amateurs. So what other conclusion am I to draw? Or is there someone in particular you just don't want to leave?'

Like Greg Peters? He couldn't have made his insinuation clearer if he'd written it in red ink on the virginal white cloth, and Fern's lips tightened mutinously as anger bubbled up inside her. She wouldn't let him ruffle her when she hadn't even done anything wrong. He was merely one of the agency's clients, albeit an important one—unfortunate though it was—and she'd handle him with the same aplomb and diplomacy with which she would handle any client.

So she answered calmly, 'Yes, Mr McManus— Harrison Stone. There's been a takeover.' Her white teeth flashed in a smile devoid of all sincerity as she dared to acquaint him with the obvious. 'Consequently, I'm not only responsible for the duties in my new position at the moment, but for a great deal of the work that's been carried over from the post I was holding before, and I value my job over and above everything else. So it would seem ludicrous for me to dump it all on to someone else while I rush off to Bermuda, especially when—as you're so reluctant to accept—I don't feel I have enough experience to do justice to ALI's location work at this stage. And as Mr Stone gave me the choice—well...' she shrugged, '... quite simply, at the moment, I just don't want to go.'

She took a long draught of her orange juice after delivering that dignified little speech, unaware of how self-possessed she appeared as she set her glass down again, or of the way those penetrating eyes were measuring the classic curve of her forehead below the honey-blonde hair and the soft line of her cheek and jaw. Suddenly, though, he was sitting forward, elbows on the table, studying her over the top of his steepled hands. And he said quietly, 'Oh, I think you will.'

The soft confidence in his voice made her turn quickly, a small knot of tension clutching at her stomach.

'As you've already stated, you value your job,' he reminded her, answering her silent query, the cruel twist to his lips turning her uneasiness almost to fear. 'Perhaps you wouldn't mind me mentioning to him exactly how I found you in my bed last Saturday?'

'You wouldn't dare...?' A quick survey of those implacable features and Fern realised she should have known better than to challenge him. He was a man who thrived on challenges—he had to be, to have acquired the multi-millionaire status so young. And something told her he would relish the prospect of contention with—and conquest over—Fern Baxter!

Above the open V of her blouse, her throat worked nervously. But she said steadily enough, even managing a dismissive, haughty little laugh, 'I hardly think he'd be interested!' Even if Connor's false accusations didn't do much to enhance her character with Franklin, he would hardly be likely to fire a member of staff for immoral behaviour outside the firm. And she could always explain her own version of the story to him herself.

A broad shoulder lifted beneath the quality grey cloth. Perhaps he'd realised that too, she thought, relieved—then tensed as he said, with the smoothness of a hot knife slicing through butter, 'But I'm interested, Fern. What makes a girl like you take on a married man in the first place? Did he spin you a sob story about his wife not understanding him? That's the usual excuse for infidelity, isn't it?'

'It wasn't like that——' she started to explain, having decided that things had already got too far out of hand, but he cut in, censure blazing through every proud angle of that striking face, through the tough, inexorable authority.

'It never is! So what were you doing? Playing tiddly-winks in my apartment?'

'No. He took me out to dinner and then we went back to the flat purely to discuss business, but things started happening that I didn't plan.'

'I'll bet they did!' His assessment cracked back at her like a whiplash. 'If that pesky little car I'd hired hadn't broken down on me coming from the airport, who knows what I might have found?'

'You've got a disgusting mind!' Angry colour burned in the pale translucency of her skin, while she wondered at whatever set of circumstances had combined to mislead her so completely about the man—even to the car he drove. 'Nothing happened! And anyway, it's no concern of yours——'

'Try telling that to him.' Disdain hardened the jaw Connor jerked towards the portly figure of her employer, who was heading back through the restaurant, filled to capacity now. Mainly businessmen on expenses, Fern deduced distractedly, from the exorbitant prices she'd noted on the menu. 'I'm sure he'll be more than interested in your sleeping habits, particularly as they happen to include his son-in-law.'

Fern stared at him, at the hard implacability of his features, shock trickling like a numbing anaesthetic along her veins. Too stunned even to express a further, immediate denial of his accusations, she could see now why Greg had told her he was married when he had! It must have thwarted all his hopes to carry on deceiving her when he'd found out that his wife's father would be working with the girl he intended to seduce!

'You've got it all wrong,' she said in an effort for self-redemption—then realised, when she saw the scepticism in the glance Connor sliced at her, that any explanation now would be totally futile. All he would think was that she was simply trying to save her job!

'Have I?' he whispered huskily, sitting back as the other man joined them again, and Fern flinched from the gleam of victory in those piercing eyes. Perhaps she could try telling Franklin the truth before Connor gave him his version of it. But she didn't think it would be that ethical, and, even if she did, would he believe her? Hopelessly she remembered those innocent lunches she had shared with Greg; the West End shows; that dinner on Saturday night. Several people in the office knew she had been seeing him—even if it had been on a purely platonic basis—and all his father-in-law had to do was ask around the agency to draw his own conclusions! Connor was right. If even the most harmless facts about her and Greg reached Franklin's ears, it could cost her her job. Like a fool, she had been entirely taken in by Greg's winning charm, unaware of his marital status, and for that piece of inane ignorance, Connor McManus seemed bent on making her pay!

She tensed, hearing Franklin's warm voice enquiring, 'And what have you two been talking about while I've been gone?'

Then the deeper one, arrogant in its victory, resonant, superbly calm. 'I don't think you need worry about

Fern's initial doubts over the Bermuda job, Franklin. Somehow I think I've managed to convince her that it would be well within her capabilities.'

Under the table she had to restrain her right foot from making contact with one very masculine shin, biting her tongue as she heard the other man congratulating Connor, while those vigilant eyes watched her, daring her to protest. He had been merely playing with her before, she realised. But he wasn't playing any more. He had the whip hand and he knew it, and if she didn't comply he'd take extreme pleasure in bringing it cracking down exactly where it hurt.

'You look pale.' Beside her, he had the audacity to be voicing concern. 'The company's obviously been working her too hard, Franklin,' he said, deliberately excluding her. 'Perhaps this trip abroad might be just the thing she needs—a chance to get away from things she clearly shouldn't be allowing to get on top of her.'

His crude insinuation was so plain—to Fern, if not to her employer—that she blushed furiously, seeing Connor's motives purely for what they were.

So it was his objective to get her away from Greg Peters, she realised dauntingly, understanding now why Connor had been so angry at finding her in his bed. Greg's wife was a long-standing friend. Longer than Greg, by the sound of it. And probably Connor thought he would be saving the woman's marriage by taking her, Fern, away, teaching her a lesson he probably felt she sorely needed! And she couldn't do a thing about it if she wanted to keep her job!

CHAPTER THREE

SOMETHING brushed her arm and Fern opened her eyes, awakening to the constant hum of the aeroplane and Connor reaching across her, his closeness startlingly intimate, bringing her pulses to life in a way that was shockingly profound.

'I didn't meant to wake you, but it's time to fasten your seatbelt,' he told her, fastening the strap deftly across her middle. 'We'll be landing soon.'

She glanced out of the window, seeing only wispy white cloud, and striving for her usual composure, her pulse still throbbing even though Connor had sat back in his seat, she uttered, 'Thanks. I didn't realise my safety was a particular concern of yours.'

Stealing a glance his way, she saw him grimace. 'Don't take it personally,' he said laconically, the deepening grooves around his eyes and mouth assuring her that if she wanted to pursue this continual cold war with him he'd be with her all the way. 'ALI, however, needs you in one piece, and while you're working for my company I intend to see to it that you stay that way until what you came here to do is done.'

'That's chivalrous of you,' she murmured, half to herself, turning to look out of the small round window again with a little inaudible sigh.

Six hours on a plane with him hadn't softened him towards her. He still believed Greg was her lover, and she'd be hanged if she'd try and convince him otherwise after he'd used the threat of getting her fired from her job simply to get her to accompany him to Bermuda!

38

Involuntarily she shivered, wondering why he had been so determined, but when she had challenged him about it earlier over coffee in the airport terminal—just the two of them, because the rest of her team were taking a later flight—he had merely reiterated what he had intimated that day at that lunch over two weeks before.

'Franklin and his daughter are close friends of mine,' he rasped, contempt for Fern stamped on every hard, beautifully chiselled feature. 'I've known Sarah since we were kids together, and I'll be darned if I'll stand by and see her marriage broken up by a self-indulgent little tramp. Not when I can step in and prevent it happening,' he'd finished with a nerve-shaking determination.

'And how exactly do you imagine you can possibly achieve that? Surely absence will only make his arms infinitely more inviting!' Fern had taunted with feigned incredulity. 'Or do you intend to keep blackmailing me to stop me seeing him even after this assignment's over?'

Anger had lit his eyes, but surprisingly calmly he had said, 'By the time this assignment's over I intend to make it my business to see that you won't want anything more to do with Greg Peters—that's a promise.'

Even now she shuddered, remembering the hard resolve in his voice, and wondering what he had meant by that last remark. But the plane was losing height, and, shaking off her uneasy thoughts, Fern gazed keenly out of the window.

Island cloud was dispersing, giving way to shimmering blue water, while Bermuda rose softly above the waves, the blend of green hills and white roof-tops of Britain's exotic tax haven standing proudly alone in the Atlantic.

'What you're seeing is the tip of a submarine mountain, extending fifteen thousand feet below the sea.' Connor's advisory tones drifted over her shoulder, all disdain shelved as he became the accommodating escort, remembering this was her first visit to Bermuda. 'The islands actually form what's left of an ancient volcano. Oh, it's all right, it's quite extinct,' he assured her with something close to amusement in his voice at her dubious expression, the austerity of his features softened by that rare spark of warmth.

As the woman he cared about would probably see him, Fern thought, cogitating over the foreign-sounding creature he had referred to at that lunch that first week of the takeover. Sabrina Bianca. She was surprised that she had even remembered the name. What was it? Spanish? Italian? And why was she even wasting time wondering? she asked herself, mentally shrugging the thought of his ladyfriend aside because they were landing now, and only minutes later, it seemed, they were stepping through Customs into the sun-drenched street.

'I forgot to mention...Ross has invited us to a party tonight,' Connor informed her when they were in the taxi, crossing a causeway that joined the air terminal with the mainland. 'It isn't normally advisable or recommended for helping jet lag, but it might be wise to get some sleep this afternoon. From past experience of Ross's parties...' He pulled a wry face, clearly well acquainted with the man who would be endorsing his company's new products, looking cool, Fern thought, in a short-sleeved shirt and lightweight trousers, while her own long-sleeved blouse and trousers that she had worn to leave a cold, drizzly England seemed to be sticking to her now.

'They're that good?' she laughed, relieved that they seemed to have shelved their differences for the time being, relaxing beneath the stunning beauty of the scenery.

Colour dominated everywhere; in the pastel-tinted houses and hotels—even the churches—with each detached limestone building crowned by the same characteristically white terraced roof; in the lush green of the hillsides, and in the bright splashes of flora—the reds and pinks and creams of the hibiscus flowers, oleander and frangipani—growing as abundantly as weeds along the wayside, where leaning palm trees fanned a welcome for the passing motorist and the obvious number of motor-scooters breezing along on the narrow road.

'Bermuda's particularly strict about traffic,' Connor told her as two motorcylists suddenly overtook them with a breath-catching gamble. 'One car per family, and no self-drive hire either—even for tourists—which is why you'll see so many mopeds on the road. The only problem arises in that most of the tourists are American, with one or two trying to compromise on our British habit of driving on the left!'

She laughed again, liking him in this mood—easy and congenial, with the corners of his eyes crinkling in amusement.

'That's not funny!' she breathed, still laughing, and gasped as they came around a bend to a panorama of pink sand, the soft, sweeping crescent of a South Shore beach, washed by an ocean of unbelievable blue. 'I don't believe this colour!' It was too much, and she held her breath, wondering if her camera could ever capture it all, and pretending not to notice Connor's smug expression—aware, as he must have been, that she was already glad she had come. She took a moment to savour the sweetness of the warm, oleander-filled air through the open window, before asking, 'Why do all the buildings have white roofs?'

His gaze slid over her face, bathed by the sun coming in on her side of the car and making his eyes appear as rich as deep, dark velvet.

'The island depends almost entirely on the rain for its water supply,' he told her with a twist of a smile, 'so every householder's responsible for catching and storing rainwater itself. The roofs are painted with a white lime-stone wash that purifies the rain as it falls. Then it's trapped by those raised gutters...' Casually he leaned over with his arm across the back of her seat, pointing out the feature on one of the little pink buildings they were passing '...and the water runs through down-spouts to a tank which is normally adjacent to or under the house.'

'I see,' she said, afraid to look at him because he was too close and her heart was beating too fast, her nostrils picking up the scent of his musky warmth that told her that, for all his cool appearance, he was as hot and sticky as she was. 'So account for the bus shelters having them as well!' suddenly she was challenging with a tremulous little laugh. 'Even that little blue telephone booth back there looked as if it had been iced!'

'It's a honeymoon island,' the driver's warm voice was elucidating with a thick Caribbean accent. 'Everything has to blend—to look nice. That's why you won't see no litter, no rust on the cars. The Government won't allow it.' He beamed at them through the rear-view mirror. 'You folks on honeymoon?' Fern was aghast to hear him suddenly asking.

'Why? Is it that apparent?' Connor was laughing down into her startled face, clearly amused by the fierce defiance he saw there as the other man chatted on obliviously.

'In Bermuda *everyone's* on honeymoon!' he extolled with an expressive gesture of his hand. 'They say if you aren't in love when you arrive, you will be by the time you leave. With the country if nothin' else!'

'Do you hear that, Fern?' Those proud, strong features were etched with derision. 'It seems there's hope for us yet.'

Sending him a look of pure disdain, Fern heard Connor laugh softly under his breath as she turned away, feeling uncomfortably warm from more than just the tropical heat, so that she was glad when the car swung on to the palm-hemmed drive of their hotel.

'I've got to go out to see someone,' Connor told her as they finished signing in, 'but I'll see you this evening. I've ordered a cab for eight-thirty.'

So he didn't intend spending any more time with her than he had to, Fern thought, piqued to realise an absurd disappointment, though she failed to understand why. After all, she could relax and enjoy her surroundings much more when he wasn't around.

And she did just that, first unpacking the case he had carried up to the antique-furnished single room for her, before going to his own on another floor. And then, tempted by the view from her window of the luxuriant gardens enclosing the moderate-sized nineteenth-century hotel, she wandered outside, to discover a private beach beyond the almond trees and the immaculate green carpet of a croquet lawn; had a swim in the practically deserted pool that beckoned invitingly beside the pastel-pink stonework of a gazebo, returning then to relax and shower before getting ready to meet Connor by eight-thirty.

Punctual to the minute, he was knocking at her door, and she was pleased to detect a catch of his breath—a chink in that armour of enviable self-poise—when he saw her.

'Well!' His breath released itself with his slow appreciation of the floating white creation that fell in soft folds across her body and wrapped itself, harem-fashion, around one slender leg and left one shoulder bare, ivory-pale against the wild tumble of magnificent blonde hair. 'You look ... very lovely.'

'So do you.' Fern didn't know why she said it. She wasn't usually so forward in complimenting a man, but in a black evening suit he looked dynamic enough to have started her pulses racing as soon as she had opened the door to him, and she only managed to retain her composure in assuming that he probably wasn't even aware of the effect he was having on her, since for once he seemed to be undergoing some inner struggle with himself.

'Are we ready?' she asked breezily, picking up a white evening bag and feeling ready for anything because she had taken his advice that afternoon and slept after she had returned from her walk.

'Surprisingly, yes.' A muscle worked beside that passionate mouth and from the emotionless cast of his features he was very much in command of himself again. 'May I congratulate you on being the only woman who's never kept me waiting?'

From him that was praise indeed, and an absurd inner warmth lent a rosy hue to her cheeks as she answered with feigned calmness, locking her door, 'Really? Perhaps you've been mixing with the wrong type of female.'

'No,' he said quietly, that dark, oddly demonic image seeming to mock her as they crossed the carpeted corridor. 'Not until now.'

His remark was like a douse of cold water after the warming effects of his compliment, but she bit her tongue, refusing to be drawn into an argument with him as he pressed the button for the lift.

Outside, the air was sweet with oleander, the chirping of crickets with the shrill whistling of tree-frogs and the thin, metallic sound of a fountain greeting them in chorus through the scented dusk.

'You don't like me very much, do you, Connor?' How on earth had that wistful note crept into her voice? She didn't give a hoot, surely?

Fortunately she was spared from hearing him spell it out because their taxi had arrived, and their driver's friendly chatter kept personal differences at bay until the car pulled up in front of a monstrous marble-pillared white house.

'Ross never could do anything in a subtle way,' Connor remarked to Fern with dry amusement at her incredulous expression as he threw her door closed behind her. 'That goes for his entire lifestyle. However, he's damn good under water and is prepared to go along with anything we want as long as we pay him enough. He's also immensely wealthy and irresistibly attractive to women, although there isn't a Mrs Walker, so I shouldn't think he'd be that much of a challenge for you.'

There it was again—that unquestioning contempt—and Fern shot him a hard glance as they passed a silent pageant of expensive cars parked on the huge semicircle of the drive. Status symbols of the rich, she thought, unconsciously pulling a face as she mounted the steps beside Connor, their footsteps a light sound, in harmony, over the marble surface.

'You never give up, do you?' she snapped, unwillingly appreciating the dark outline of that sweeping brow, the near-noble nose and strongly defined jaw, the sheer masculinity of him taking her breath away.

'When I set my mind on something—never.' His satin-smooth response caused her pulse to gather momentum, and she almost missed her footing, feeling his steadying fingers instantaneously at her elbow, sensing his closeness so profoundly for a split second that her body raced with sensations that inwardly shook her.

What had he meant by that? Tremulously, she started to say something, stopping short because someone had opened the massive cedar door, spilling light down over the steps, drawing them into a party that was already in full swing.

'Connor! Glad you could make it.' From out of the crowd a tall, blond man in a white dinner-jacket emerged. Their host, Fern guessed, and from her first glance at the gelled-back hair and the waxy perfection of his features she assessed that he had to be a few years younger than Connor. 'And *who* is this?'

A pair of stripping blue eyes immediately warned Fern that Ross Walker was a womaniser, and he was certainly an attractive man, although there was something rather blatant about him—like his house, she decided, absorbing a spectacle of chandeliers, indoor waterfalls and ornate ponds around which some guests were dancing to a live trio. She gave him her best smile, though, as Connor made the introductions, and felt his eyes on her, sharp as an eagle's, as she shook hands with the younger man.

'Fern's simply working with you—just remember that,' Connor cautioned with a lop-sided smile, but Fern sensed there was more meaning behind that warning than he was allowing to show—one that advised Ross to keep away.

Why? Because he thought her morally corrupt?

Her lips compressing with annoyance, she caught the glimmer of laughter in Connor's eyes, and something else—something unmistakably feral—as Ross laid sudden claim to her with an arm about her shoulders, breathing in an accent that was, she decided, a strange mixture of Australian and southern States, 'One thing's for sure—she's too young for you, Connor, unless you've suddenly taken to cradle-snatching.' Fern controlled a long-suffering sigh. Yet again someone else under the same

misconception about her age. 'There's plenty of time to
talk business later, my lovely,' Ross was addressing her
through a hullabaloo of laughter and music and conversation. 'First let me drag you away from this satanic-
looking devil who's trying to keep you all to himself and
allow me to drown you in champagne.'

Fern laughed, warming to Ross Walker in spite of
herself. As long as she kept them at arm's length, she
assured herself from experience, she could always handle
men like him. But as for Connor... A small shiver passed
through her, strangely at variance with the heat of the
semi-tropical night. And as for him wanting to keep her
to himself—Ross had to be mistaken, surely? she
thought, considering how much he despised her. Yet still
a sudden, uneasy tension etched her fine features as she
remembered what he had said to her outside.

'She'll tell you she doesn't drink.' Connor's perfect
English tones cut into her disturbing thoughts, sardonic
against the strong beat of a recent number one hit.
'However, ply her with what you will, Ross, the lady's
still leaving with me.' And when they both looked at
him, Ross with friendly arrogance, Fern with rebellion,
he added, command in every line of that dark, imposing
physique, 'I'm picking up the tab on this assignment,
remember, and I don't intend losing any time through
all-night parties and hangovers—which means I'm
making myself responsible for seeing Fern gets to bed
on time.'

Just who did he think he was? Fern glared at him in
open defiance, which was met by such a resolute promise
in those dark eyes that Ross laughed out loud as he led
her away.

'What is it with him?' he said drily. 'I've never seen
him in such a possessive mood.'

'Don't worry.' Still bristling from Connor's audacity,
she flashed Ross a brilliant smile, aware that Harrison

Stone's prestigious client was still watching her as she let the other man guide her towards the glitteringly mirrored bar. 'I can assure you it isn't possessiveness,' she stressed, privately marvelling at the vast display of marine relics, some probably worth a fortune, adorning every wall and shelf and alcove—sad, silent anachronisms, she thought, in that outrageous shrine to modern wealth. 'He's only concerned with getting the job done. As he said, he's paying for it. And I suppose if I were in his shoes I'd be judicious too,' she laughed, 'knowing the rates we charge!'

'He can afford it.' On the brink of refusing, gingerly, Fern took the glass Ross had procured from a passing member of his bar staff, changing her mind. It wasn't every day she came to Bermuda, so why not celebrate with one glass of champagne? 'He might not show it off in quite the same way as I do, but, if no one's told you, Connor McManus is a walking phenomenon. He pays more in taxes in six months than most men earn in a lifetime, and he's totally self-made—had to work like the devil to get where he is today—unlike some of us who were just born lucky.' Meaning that Ross Walker had never had to take a job seriously in his life, Fern interpreted, remembering Franklin telling her last week that the treasure-hunter was the only son of one of Australia's metal-mining magnates—that he was a playboy in the true sense, having casinoed and race-tracked his way round Europe and America before settling down to wreck exploring there in Bermuda. 'And you're a naïve little thing if you think he was only talking about the assignment over there just now. I only hope you're experienced enough to know how to manage a man like that. He's got his hooks into you like an angler into a beautiful blue marlin, so you'd better just watch he doesn't yank the line in and you find yourself stranded on deck before he cuts you loose.'

Fern smiled wanly, her skin feeling tight and stretched. Connor wasn't interested in her any more than she was in him, she told herself with a none the less sudden quickening of her blood, because she couldn't forget what he had said on the way in here tonight, or the look in his eyes before Ross had led her away. And Ross had called her naïve! What a joke, she thought, when Connor only saw her as an immoral little tramp whom he imagined he had dragged reluctantly away from her married lover's arms!

'I'm older than you think,' she purred sweetly, smiling up at him as she sipped at her champagne, and, glancing across the room, saw Connor, standing with several other guests, those dark eyes burning with unveiled anger in her direction. She stiffened, tension coiling like a spring inside her as she felt the pull of that devastating male magnetism like a tide under the powerful influence of the moon. But then someone touched his arm, a chignoned, dusky-skinned beauty in a slinky blue dress whose model-fine bone-structure and dazzling smile were more than enough to distract him and break the waves of electricity Fern had felt coming across the floor.

'That's Madree.' Ross was answering the question that had scarcely been formed in Fern's mind. 'Stunning, isn't she? Her father's an American lawyer who plucked a dark jewel off the island—and Madree's the result. She's the model who'll be working with us on ALI's ad work. I think Connor's used her before.'

'How nice for Connor,' Fern breathed with feigned sweetness, placing a hand swiftly over her glass as Ross tried to refill it from the bottle he had just secured from a passing waiter. Was she the 'someone' he had been so impatient to see that afternoon?

'I'd imagined his hands were pretty full at the moment,' he remarked, filling his own glass, his blue gaze lifting from the clear, pale liquid to rove appreciatively over Fern.

She shook her head, her hair falling softly over the pale cream of her shoulder. 'You've got it all wrong, Ross,' she laughed—then wished she hadn't when he moved closer, more confident in discovering the field was clear.

Well, it was, she thought. As far as Connor McManus was concerned! Madree could keep him fully entertained while he was here for all she cared! And she'd already guessed—if the Mediterranean-sounding little dish he obviously kept hot back in England was anything to go by—that he liked his women dark and exotic. Which ruled her out for a start!

She couldn't understand why the party had suddenly lost all its earlier appeal, covering her glass again as Ross seemed bent on tempting her with more champagne, stiffening a little as his arm suddenly slid around her shoulders and he plunged into an account of his latest underwater acquisitions.

Across the room Madree was sparkling in Connor's company, talking, smiling, her liquid brown eyes upturned to his, and yet though he appeared to be listening to whatever the model was saying his gaze was fixed intently on Fern.

So why should he object to her showing an interest in Ross Walker? she wondered, seeing the dark censure manifested in his face. Wasn't it his intention that she should forget Greg in his entirely erroneous conjecture that she was Greg's mistress? Well, let him object! she thought tightly, trying to absorb herself then in something Ross was telling her about wreck exploring—clearly his pet topic! she realised somewhat wearily after a while, annoyed to feel her heart skip a beat as she heard Connor's voice just behind her.

'I think it wise to remind you that we aren't in Bermuda entirely to enjoy ourselves,' he aimed directly at Fern, the hard angles of his face marked by cool intolerance. 'Don't you think one of us ought to start thinking about getting the job organised?'

Piqued by his flaying authority, Fern had to bite her tongue. He was obviously angry because she was getting on so well with Ross, she guessed, aware of the swift withdrawal of the arm around her shoulders as soon as Connor had appeared at her side. However, that didn't give him the right to speak to her as if she were incompetent! she fumed silently. And until Jenny, their liaison girl, and the rest of the team, arrived tomorrow, any arrangements on behalf of Harrison Stone were her responsibility, not his!

'I was going to suggest it an hour ago,' she explained none the less affably for Ross's sake, 'but you seemed to be too tied up.' This with an unwitting glance towards a lifelike configuration of brass nudes in some rather mind-boggling poses near where she had last seen him talking to the model.

She flinched, realising that he had noticed when his eyes mocked that waspish note she had been unable to contain and he said phlegmatically, 'Madree went home. I asked her to stay and meet you, but she said she hoped you'd excuse her. She's had a particularly exhausting afternoon.'

I'll bet she has! Fern thought, with a giddying surge of emotion, but controlled it enough to say sweetly, 'How unfortunate! And I was dying to meet her too. But I hope you didn't feel you had to desert the poor girl just because of me,' and, in a reckless endeavour to nettle him because of his cutting remarks a moment ago, she sent a blazing smile up at the tall, blond man beside her, adding, 'Ross was looking after me *very* well.'

The way those brown eyes impaled her made her heart thud over the slow, deep rhythm of the band's lead singer that was suddenly drifting across the room.

She had got to him, she thought smugly, seeing the way his jaw and cheekbones seemed to stand out beneath the tautness of his skin, wishing she hadn't when his fingers suddenly clamped painfully on to her lower arm and he said in a way that was more of a statement than a request, 'You won't mind if I take Fern away from you now, will you, Ross? We've got a lot to discuss. And if you can manage to wind this party up before midnight tomorrow, we'll meet you as arranged the following morning at ten-thirty sharp.'

Sanguinely, Fern prayed for an immediate demur from Ross, but got only his laughing acquiescence as Connor urged her towards the other couples who were swaying, arms entwined, to the romantic song.

'And suppose I object?' Hot colour touched her cheeks. She wished Ross had raised his own objection to that arrogant assertion of Connor's, instead of standing there jokingly complying. That was the basic difference, though, between the playboy and the man who built empires, she guessed. The emperor was used to commanding, controlling others. The playboy wasn't.

'Oh, I don't think you will.' Those heavy lids were lowered, concealing his innermost thoughts, but she could feel the tension pulsing through every hard inch of him as he gazed down at her from his superior height.

'Why?' She gave a small gasp of awareness as he pulled her determinedly against him, her own pulse leaping, her voice faltering, uncontrolled. 'Because you'll tell Franklin your sordid little story about me if I do?'

He merely smiled, a lazy, vulpine smile. 'You've really got a low opinion of me, haven't you?' His voice was soft, disturbingly seductive against the deep, resonant notes of the male vocals, as seductive as his warmth and the spicy freshness of his cologne.

'You're quick to catch on,' Fern uttered, yet shakily, suddenly profoundly aware of the intense male aura of raw sexuality surrounding him.

A muscle pulled beside his jaw and his mouth took on lines that were almost frighteningly grim. 'And I was under the impression that you didn't mind who man-handled you, since you seemed to be enjoying it so much with Ross.'

It was only the very public situation that stopped her hand from making contact with his arrogant face, her body tense with restraint as she snapped back, 'Only because Ross isn't an overbearing oaf, and when it comes to knowing how to treat a woman he could probably beat you hands down!'

'Want to bet?'

Suddenly her feet weren't in time with the music and, unbalanced, she swayed, catching her breath from a plethora of sensations as his arm tightened around her, steadying her against the long, hard warmth of his body. Her senses swam, her body tingling, her breasts aching in rounded tumescence against the hard wall of his chest. But of course, she thought headily, he was right. She didn't need a degree in psychology to know that men like Ross Walker were usually plastic beneath the surface, and that if she had to put her trust, her reliance, in Ross or Connor, she was surprised to acknowledge that, in-stinctively, she would choose Connor.

'What exactly do you want?' she breathed, non-plussed by her own reluctant assessment of his character, her eyes meeting his, guarded and uncertain.

He touched his cheek to her temple, the compara-tively rough texture of his skin against hers exciting her, causing her blood to race. Her fingertips were startlingly red against the dark fabric of his jacket—female complementing male—in their mere token of an effort to hold him at bay, and her heart was hammering as she became shockingly conscious of the way their bodies fitted so well together, hip against hip, thigh against thigh, the deep rhythm of his breathing assuring her how much more in control he was than she, as he said quietly, 'Perhaps what Greg Peters finds irresistible enough to cheat on his wife for.'

Fern's head jerked up in a cascade of gold under the light of the chandeliers, her senses electrified by the mental pictures his words conveyed. 'Then you'll just have to keep wanting, won't you, Connor?' somehow she managed to utter in trembling response.

'Will I?' His smile was confident—insolent—and she sucked in her breath as his hand lifted to caress the soft exposed flesh of her shoulder, every nerve tingling from the devastating and unwelcome response his touch produced in her. 'Tell me, do you always look so inviting when a man holds you in his arms?' His words breathed a gentle caress against her hair. 'Is that the way you enslaved poor Greg, with those lovely flushed cheeks and those bright hazel eyes, and that soft, irresistible mouth?'

Desire, fierce and undisguised, lit the gaze that burned across her lips, and her heart thudded as for one crazy moment she thought he was going to kiss her. But then he laughed softly at the shocked defiance in her face, an almost contemptuous mockery back in his, saying suddenly, 'Very soon you can show me how well your artistic theories work in practice. I've arranged for us to meet the best underwater photographer I know in Hamilton tomorrow—which should also give us time for some sightseeing, and that should give my staff a day to get all the equipment and materials you'll need for the first session on to the *Host* for the following day.'

His abrupt transition from pleasure to business was startling to say the least, and it took her a few moments to pull herself out of the sensual web he had insidiously woven around her.

'Thanks,' she said, with a quiver in her voice, realising through fogged sensibilities that he was referring to his company yacht which he had arranged for her agency to make use of as a background for the surface shots of ALI's new products, and which was permanently moored in Bermuda.

The assignment was all he seemed to want to discuss, then and on the journey back to their hotel, leaving her with only a courteous 'goodnight,' as he let her out of the lift on her floor to travel on up to his own.

In bed, Fern tossed and turned, wondering if he'd said what he had when they were dancing because he fully intended to seduce her, or simply because he wanted to see her reaction, to unsettle her—despising her as he did because he thought she was having an affair with Greg. Well, it had, and he knew it, she thought, berating herself for the traitorous responses of her body when he had held her in his arms, suggesting that they might possibly be lovers. How could she even welcome such an idea? she asked herself incredulously, because even now the thought of physical surrender to Connor McManus made her pulse-rate quicken, putting a sick and throbbing fever into her blood. And heaven knew how! But on that thought she must have fallen asleep, because the next thing she knew the phone was ringing beside her bed and broken sunlight was spilling through the slats of the venetian blind.

CHAPTER FOUR

'YOU lazy little thing, don't you know it's nine forty-five?' Connor's deep voice trickled amusement into Fern's drowsy ear. 'Skip breakfast,' he advised after her first shocked gasp of horror over her alarm having failed to go off. 'We'll get something in Hamilton. There's a ferry leaving in thirty minutes. I'll see you down in the lobby in twenty-five.'

The line going dead robbed her of any chance to object. Not that she wanted to, despite the fact that they weren't seeing the photographer until later that afternoon, because she desperately wanted to see all she could of Bermuda—even if Connor's invitation had been more of an order than a request. So she was rather pleased with herself when, dressed in a navy blue and white polka-dot sundress, her hair twisted into a topknot and wearing only a trace of lipstick and mascara, she arrived downstairs still with several minutes to spare.

'I'm impressed,' he said, his mouth firming in approval as she came up to him standing in the cool luxury of the foyer.

'That was the idea.' There was just an edge of tartness to her voice that caused those dark irises to glitter with something challenging. But then, catching her elbow, he said briskly, 'Come on. We can just make it if we hurry.'

They did. Sitting beside him in the welcoming shade of the canopied cruiser, Fern was acutely conscious of the female looks Connor was attracting, and she could appreciate why. In the palest blue shirt and light trousers, he epitomised masculinity at its best, lean, lithe and extremely fit, with the sea breezes ruffling his hair and that carved mouth almost saturnine as he gazed past her, seawards, and, despite knowing how much he despised her, she couldn't deny that it felt good being with a man who could turn so many women's heads.

She was grateful for the view that drew her own attention away from him, to the sparkling water of the Great Sound and the many diminutive islands they were passing. White-roofed mansions peeped shyly through closeting foliage, or stood proud like vainglorious palaces—homes of the rich and famous seeking seclusion from a curious, prying world. A speedboat overtook them, its engine burring, pulling a water-skier in a blaze of silver spray, while in the distance, in the open channel leading out into the ocean, a yacht dipped and rose, white sails stretched, full blown by the strength of the cooling crosswinds.

'You mentioned you sailed.'

She started, Connor's sudden remark imparting that he had been conscious of her interest. 'Yes,' she reaffirmed, tasting the salt of sea-spray on her lips, remembering telling him on the plane that she'd spent most of her weekends as a child sailing with her parents. 'Dad took early retirement recently,' she went on to tell him now, 'and they've bought a house near Lake Windermere so that they can sail every day. I haven't been up to see it yet.'

'Are you an only child?'

She nodded, and from under her lashes noticed the way he was watching her—with a hard discernment that prompted her to add, 'What are you thinking? That I've probably been spoilt?'

And instantly regretted it when he drawled in a voice that was warm, if anything, holding no trace of acerbity, 'I wasn't thinking anything of the sort.'

She was being unusually tetchy. Probably, she guessed, because she half expected him always to be thinking the worst about her, to respond with some flaying comment—and she bit her lip, her gaze clashing so directly with the hard brilliance of his that an unexpected little thrill ran through her. 'What about you?' Suddenly she felt a burning curiosity to know everything about him, aware that up until now he had given away very little about himself, and yet she experienced an absurd shyness to be asking, 'Have you any family?'

He brought one leg up over the other, clasping his knee. 'I've got a married sister with two children, and a brilliant college professor for a brother-in-law. I've also got a widowed father of eighty-two.'

'Eighty-two!' Amazement lit Fern's face, and she looked at him, half expecting some sign that he was joking. Even if he were ten years older it would still have been a vast generation gap!

He smiled wryly, obviously aware of what she was thinking. 'He was nearly thirty years older than my mother,' he explained, raking back a wind-blown strand of hair from his face, 'but they had a good marriage. She died young.'

'I'm sorry.' Detecting the regret in his voice, Fern didn't know what else to say, and she spent a few moments thinking about that reference he had made to his brother-in-law being a college professor. Was it the same college that this . . . Sabrina attended? Was that how she and Connor had met? Above the boat a sea-bird soared—a long-tailed gull, its black-tipped wings silver-streaked by the sun as it circled, swooping low across the water towards the gently rising hillside of the mainland.

'I try to keep an eye on my father as often as I can, but he's in good health and very independent,' Connor was conveying with definite gratitude in his voice, 'and determined to live alone! He spends most of his time these days playing golf and ballroom dancing.'

'Ballroom dancing!' laughed Fern, enjoying this new rapport with him, only vaguely conscious of other people around them—a young couple with a gurgling baby, sitting opposite on the long front seat; a businessman in jacket and grey flannel Bermudas; the click of a camera as someone took photographs across the walkway. 'He sounds like a real character!'

'He is.'

It was evident, too, that Connor was very fond of him, Fern thought, surprised to realise that he was such a family man, remembering then that ball she had noticed in his garden to which she had attached very detrimental significance at the time. Had it belonged to a niece—a nephew, perhaps?

Trying to dispel an oddly disturbing mental picture of him indulging in a light-hearted game with children, she was brought out of her reverie by him asking, 'Have you read *The Wizard of Oz*?'

'What?'

His gaze had shifted, lifting past her, then back again with lazy amusement at her puzzled smile. 'You see that house on that island over there?'

Profoundly conscious of his knee casually brushing hers, she followed the jerk of his chin towards the pale, one-storey building with a curious-looking round tower, where green window shutters were drawn down against the Bermudian sun. 'It's reputed that some of the Oz characters were created in that tower—and one can believe it. Locked away up there with the right sort of... inspiration...' that briefest hesitation brought her head round to meet the startling sensuality of his smile '...who knows what a man could be galvanised into producing?'

Annoyingly, she blushed, turning back to stare at the tower, which was becoming further away now with each swell of the waves.

'Looking for happiness, Fern? For your yellow-brick road?' His voice mocked, but softly, bringing a ridiculous moistness to her eyes.

Dorothy in *The Wizard of Oz* hadn't found it—not chasing rainbows, anyway. So why did she feel like crying? Disappointment, because she'd thought she had found it with Greg? Or was she, for some absurd reason, ludicrously affected by that fragment of sensitivity she had almost imagined in Connor?

'And that's Hamilton.'

Blinking back her tears, the wind tugging at her hair, Fern turned her interest across to the other side of the boat and the capital. To the imposing hulks of two cruise ships lined up against the quay; to the yachts and cruisers moored against a backdrop of multi-roomed hotels; to the colourful Colonial buildings and the Gothic tower of a cathedral standing out against the skyline—the only grey structure in a metropolis of colour and which somehow didn't quite seem to belong, and, on the quay itself, the hugely dominating building of the country's national bank, an impressive statement of Bermuda's status as one of the financial centres of the world.

'Holy smoke!' It was all she could say at first, totally overwhelmed. 'Everything looks so *clean*!' she expressed in wonder, knowing that the dazzling white rooftops went a long way to creating that effect.

'So it should. It's the cleanest country in the world,' Connor told her with the impassivity of one used to its luxuries—the playgrounds of its jet-set. Then, 'Glad you came?' he taunted with that mocking smile, not expecting an answer, not needing one.

*   *   *

They spent the next hour or so browsing around the city, after Fern's insistence that she wasn't dying of starvation and that she wanted to see at least a little of Hamilton before they stopped to eat.

'Not even *here*!' she laughed, as they turned along one street and she recognised the familiar green and gold lettering of her favourite English chain store. Already she had noticed a shop on the Front devoted exclusively to Irish linen, others flying Union Jacks in a proud statement of their country's allegiance to the British Crown.

'It's still a British colony—in fact, it's our oldest,' Connor enlightened her, 'even if it does feel more American than English. But a fair number of people here have a fierce passion to be independent, of either country. They don't even think of themselves as Caribbean—and it's probably being seven hundred miles from any other neighbouring land or island that gives Bermuda that feeling of total uniqueness.'

Which it did, Fern thought, when they were sitting in the sweltering heat of a balcony restaurant on Front Street, looking down the palm-lined promenade. Mopeds buzzed past beside the bright Colonial shops, weaving in and out between the camper-style taxis and the gleaming Japanese saloons. Under a canopy immediately across the street, sheltering from the afternoon sun, men in Bermuda shorts and white hats waited beside their horse-drawn carriages to give rides to the tourists. Bermudians browsed or went about their business, black and white mingling with almost laid-back affability, the whole scene dominated by the huge bulk of the two cruise liners Fern had seen from out in the harbour, their passengers coming and going, their awnings fluttering in the breeze.

'Here's one experience you'll never forget about Bermuda,' Connor relayed, sharing a conspiratorial smile with the pretty waitress who was just putting two steaming bowls on their table. 'It's the marinade of hot peppers and sherry that makes it special,' he grinned as the girl poured a small amount of each mixture from two decanters into the delicious-smelling chowder he had recommended, her breathed 'You're welcome,' after his charm-emblazoned thanks just another example, Fern realised, of his devastating effect on women. 'Let me know what you think.'

Dismissing the resolute thought that it meant nothing to her who looked at him, she did as he suggested, then gasped as her first taste of the chowder seemed to explode on her tongue. 'Phew! Why didn't you warn me?' she scolded laughingly, her mouth burning from the zing of the peppers, the unexpected kick of the sherry.

'And miss that marvellous reaction?' He was laughing with her, his teeth strong and white against the healthy olive of his skin. 'You know, you're really very beautiful,' he said, his gaze raking disconcertingly over the gentle contours of her face—over her hair, wild and wind-tossed from the ferry crossing. 'It's that look of innocence that deceives a man. Tell me, Fern, have you ever been really in love with anyone? Someone who was free to be able to return that love?'

Unaccountably, her heartbeat doubled its pace. Was he asking simply because he thought she was having an affair with Greg, or did he see himself...?

'No,' she answered truthfully, not liking the path her thoughts had suddenly taken, unable to resist adding with blatant directness, 'Have you?' just as the long, low boom from a funnel of one of the liners across the street resounded along the promenade.

'It's probably sailing at two.' Connor dropped a glance to his watch, smiling wryly at the way it had made her jump. 'Any passengers who aren't back on board will have heard it and will be frantically scrambling to pay for their souvenirs and get out of the stores before they get left behind. And in answer to your question—it's hard to reach thirty-five and not to have fallen prey to such weakness at some time or other,' he stated with cold disregard, before tucking into his soup.

So he considered love a weakness, Fern thought, buttering a piece of french toast, wondering why he had sounded so cynical. But he didn't say anything further on the subject, resorting to discussing business as their crab salads arrived, and then it was time to meet the underwater photographer to sort out the venue for the coming week, so that it was well into the afternoon before they left the studio for the ferry and the conversation returned to a more personal level again.

They had dinner with Jenny Evans and Tony Hughes from the agency, who had arrived earlier that afternoon.

In a dark suit, Connor looked dynamic, Fern thought—lean and fit in contrast to the portly stills photographer, especially since Tony was only a few years older than their wealthy client. And obviously Jenny thought the same thing, she realised a little later when they were enjoying cocktails on the terrace, because, with the two men deep in conversation, her colleague suddenly leaned across the ornate ironwork of their table and whispered, so that the others couldn't hear, 'Wow! Now I know why you arrived a day early! And all I get lumbered with is Tony!'

'For heaven's sake, Jenny! It was only for business reasons,' Fern laughed quietly back at the pretty, envying brunette. Even so, a warmth pervaded her blood because until now she hadn't realised just how much she had enjoyed the day, and, apart from that cynical remark of Connor's in the restaurant at lunchtime, they had seemed to get on very well.

'Won't you two share the joke?'

Ever vigilant, he had picked up on their whispered laughter, that dark, predatory image intensified by the flickering shadows from the glass-held candle in the centre of their table.

'Fern was just telling me what a wonderful day you two have had!' Jenny responded too eagerly, trying, as always, to get her involved with someone, Fern realised, blushing to the roots of her hair.

'Was she now? And what did she tell you?' Though she deliberately avoided looking at Connor, she could feel that mocking curiosity in his eyes, and was relieved when Tony put in with assumed authority, imitating Franklin, 'I hope she looked after you all right. Or has she been shirking on the job?'

'On the contrary.' That deep voice caressed, warm as the night breeze across her shoulders beneath the fine straps of her dress. 'She took me to Hamilton,' Connor drawled, though from that shatteringly personal smile he gave her he hadn't forgotten it was virtually the other way round! 'Then she spent the rest of the morning dragging me round the shops.'

And that wasn't completely true either, Fern remembered, because he'd searched hard for those two tiny bracelets he'd bought before they had caught the return ferry, the trouble he had taken over those gifts for his little nieces touching her with surprising acuteness.

'A typical woman,' Tony complained amiably, and turning to Fern with a knowing little wink said, 'Buy something special for Greg?'

It was the worst thing he could have said. Across the table she saw those dark eyes narrow into cold, penetrating slits, Tony's innocent remark effectively killing what small degree of warmth he might have been harbouring towards her all day. He knew she hadn't bought anything for the other man, but that didn't stop him still thinking that she was sleeping with him, she fumed silently, anger and the reckless confidence of one Planter's rum punch inciting her to respond, 'No. What I want to give Greg doesn't come in the shape of any souvenir,' her bitterness well hidden beneath a deliberately provocative smile.

'Wa-hey! Lucky bloke!' Above the sound of a car turning into the small parking area under the terrace, Tony's remark was a classic misinterpretation. And it might have pleased her if she hadn't seen the grim strength of anger that darkened on Connor's face, stripping her confidence raw, and, with an intuitive little voice warning her that she'd be wise to leave things there, she jumped up, saying with a strained casualness, 'Well, I hope nobody minds, but I'm going to bed.'

She'd deal with his mood in the morning, she decided, crossing the deserted lounge, by which time he would have cooled off considerably. Only what she hadn't reckoned on was that he would follow her, and she gave a small strangled cry as a strong hand caught her arm, whirling her round to meet the devastating anger pulsing through him.

'What the hell do you think you're doing, flaunting your cheap morals in my face—and in front of the others? Do they know he's married?' he quizzed with an angry toss of his chin towards the terrace. 'Or does everyone at Harrison Stone condone jumping in and out of bed with anyone's partner regardless?'

His fingers bruised and she winced, trying to twist free. 'You're detestable!' she spat, because Tony didn't know, and, until after the episode in Greg's flat, neither had Jenny. They were her friends, and she'd be hanged if she'd stand by and let him accuse *them* of depravity as well, flinging back unthinkingly, 'It's hardly anyone else's fault if Sarah Stone can't hang on to her husband! And from the innuendoes I've been getting from you, perhaps that isn't the problem. What's really getting to you,

Connor? The fact that I'd prefer him any day to a man like you?'

His eyes burned with a savageness that made her realise she had overstepped the mark, and his nails dug painfully into her arm. But then, surprisingly, he released her, and she realised why as a waiter appeared, to announce that there was a young lady waiting to see Connor in the foyer.

'We'll finish this later,' he promised, resolve in the grim gaze that took in her sparkling eyes and flushed cheeks before he strode away. Presumably to meet his little model, Fern decided virulently, and with a sudden sharp twist of regret she wondered where that fragile rapport between them had gone.

She couldn't sleep, try though she did, full of remorse at having been stupid enough to strengthen Connor's suspicions about her and Greg still further. She should have called his bluff, she realised, when he'd tried to insist she come here—taken her chance that he wouldn't have told Franklin what he suspected—or, if he had, that the man might have believed her side of the story over that of his friend and colleague, although she strongly doubted it. He would have imagined, like Connor, that she was simply trying to protect her job. And now here she was, in Bermuda, with a man who thoroughly despised her and yet who disturbed her equanimity beyond belief! All because she'd been too proud and angry to tell him the truth in the beginning!

The fan on the ceiling seemed to spin with her overactive brain, a soft continuous whirr of blades cutting through the heat of the night. Eventually, when sleep continued to elude her, she slipped on some light culottes and a thin top and, seeing only the night porter as she came down through the foyer, wandered out into the grounds.

Every tree and bush was alive with sound, the shrill, clear whistles of the crickets, lizards and tree-frogs ringing softly through the humid summer night. Lanterns placed high in the palms gently lit the rambling paths, illuminating a bronze statue of a nymph beside a tinkling cascade of water, perfect in its artistic detail. Light, too, spilled gently over the pink walls of the hotel's Waterfront Restaurant nestling, closed and silent now, beneath the almond trees, its sloping white roof glistening under the light of a pale full moon.

Like snow, Fern decided, entranced, except that the fronds of a date palm, stirring gently on the night breeze, intruded across her vision, and the quiet wash of the waves on the small private beach mocked her fanciful thinking.

There was no sign or sound of anyone else around. She was probably the only person to be plagued by insomnia in paradise, she thought with a grimace, tripping lightly down some steps and coming upon a small wharf overlooking the vast dark waters of the Great Sound. Lights twinkled through the darkness from scattered buildings on the other side. Small boats rocked on their moorings, and then there came more familiar tones, woven with sarcasm, cutting, with arrow-pointed precision, through the enchanted night.

CHAPTER FIVE

'MISSING him already?'

Startled, Fern swung round, Connor's words piercing through her like the beam of the lighthouse piercing through the darkness on the other side of the Sound.

'I—I didn't hear you coming.' A discernible tremor in her voice betrayed the way her pulses were racing as she saw him move out of the shadows in the white shirt and dark trousers he had been wearing earlier, his shoes making no sound on the steps that brought him down to the tiny wharf. 'I couldn't sleep.' It was the wrong thing to say, she realised, when strong grooves etched features already harshened by the effects of the lamps in the trees behind them, slashing light and shade across his face.

'I wonder why.' He moved along the quiet dockside towards her, his deep tones hanging intimidatingly on the air. 'What is it now? A week—two weeks since you saw him? Does he keep you satisfied enough that you get withdrawal symptoms if you don't see him for a mere matter of days?' Cold cynicism laced his tone, bringing goose-bumps to her flesh in spite of the warm night. 'Pity. You're going to have to get used to that when he eventually decides he prefers his wife to his latest little fling—as he invariably does, Fern. So why not start behaving like a more responsible adult and accept that he's got priorities over and above you?'

She'd been about to hit him with the truth once and for all, but his revelation that Greg had had other women shocked her speechless for a moment. Silently, however, she admitted that she should have guessed as much. Men like Greg took their opportunities where they could. Smarting, though, from the cruel lash of Connor's tongue when she was totally blameless of any immoral liaison with the other man, she was retaliating heedlessly, 'Drop dead, Connor! You think you know it all, but you don't. And anyway, you can tell Franklin Stone whatever you like, because the long and the short of it is I'm not answerable to you!'

That wasn't what she had intended to say at all, and she despaired at her own impetuosity, particularly when Connor clicked his tongue disapprovingly, and in a voice that was softly taunting queried, 'Frustration making you snappy?' He took a step nearer, saying in suddenly silken tones, 'Perhaps I can help.'

Tension crept through her like a dark, insidious traitor, and she nervously licked her lips, feeling the threat of that powerful sexuality as tangibly as the warm wind on her bare skin. If she could have swept past him easily then she would have done so, but there wasn't enough room between him and the wharf-edge to go around him safely, and he was blocking her immediate pathway to the steps.

Instead, trying to appear calm, though her heart felt as though it was going to pound right out of her body, she said, 'There's only one thing you're forgetting, Connor.' Was that really her voice sounding so matter-of-fact, so calm? 'You already said on the day we met that I wasn't your type—and you certainly aren't mine! I wouldn't get involved with you if you came gift-wrapped with silver ribbons!'

He laughed softly, his teeth glinting white in the pale light of the moon. 'I wonder.'

A tremor of fear shivered down Fern's spine and tiny beads of perspiration dampened her skin. Way off an owl hooted, an achingly lonely sound above the quiet lapping of the water against the jetty wall.

'Just because you didn't score with Madree, don't think you can come back here and find a willing substitute in me,' she told him with cool disdain, though that vibrant animal energy she could feel exuding from him was sending strange tingles along her nerve-endings.

His mouth moved in wry contemplation as the breeze teased a few gold strands across her face, carrying with it the evocative sweet scent of oleander. 'You? A substitute for Madree? Hardly,' he drawled, and now his lips twisted with something akin to distaste. 'Madree's a friend.'

'And worthy of more respect,' Fern supplied aridly, noticing how the moon streaked light across his hair, midnight-black against the jewelled velvet of the sky. Absently she saw him slip his hands into his pockets, and the action drew her gaze unconsciously to the lean, hard fitness of his waist and hips.

'Yes,' he replied with brutal honesty. 'But respect isn't what we're talking about, is it, Fern?' The sensual undertones in the resonant voice tested her already over-stretched nerves, and cautiously she took a step back, suddenly, inexplicably, afraid.

'And what about *Honey*?' she asked with sickly-sweet emphasis, saying anything to curb that festering desire she saw in him now—a desire solely to punish, to humiliate. Her throat contracting, she saw the deep cleft that appeared between his eyes, giving a harder cast to the strong planes and angles of his face. Perhaps he didn't like being reminded of the woman he had left in England when he was footloose abroad, she thought caustically, and gleaned a sick satisfaction in attempting to topple that tower of arrogant superiority by underlining his own lack of principles in flinging at him, 'You know—Sabrina

Bianca? Brain of Britain? The one who's hoping to leave college with honours at the end of the year!'

For a moment he looked decidedly...what? she wondered. Surprised, that she had even dared to mention his private life?

A fish jumped in the water a few feet away, and the soft splash impinged on her senses as Connor's mouth took on that familiar sardonic curve.

'I don't think...Sabrina worries too much about the other women in my life. She makes no demands in that respect. So don't worry, Fern, I'm totally uncommitted. But if I weren't——' his voice had grown dangerously soft against the shrill, incessant whistling of the tree-frogs '—since when would that ever bother you?'

Incensed, she curbed a swift retort as he drew a step nearer, fear overriding her anger.

'For goodness' sake, Connor! I didn't go to bed with Greg. I told you I——'

'You went out with him, didn't you?'

'Yes, but it was——'

'Every time he happened to be in London? Lunches. Dinners. The theatre.'

'Yes, but...' Her sentence tailed off. He'd really done his homework since that night he had caught her in his bed!

'And you didn't think twice about going back to my apartment with him.'

'No! I mean yes. Oh, what's the use?' Her shoulders sagged in exasperated defeat. He wouldn't listen. 'I don't have to take this from you!' she spat, fearful of that savage angry heat glittering in the coal-dark depths of his eyes. But as she made to push past him, his arm shot out to restrain her, and she let out a small cry as he dragged her back against him.

'Let go of me!' Her senses reeled from the electrifying sensation of being crushed against his hard warmth, from

the subjugation by his strength and a sudden swift punishing anger as his mouth claimed hers in bruising, in-
escapable possession.

For wild seconds she struggled, which only incited him
to tighten his hold on her, his arms securing around her
slender body like relentless bars.

With brutal expertise he forced her lips apart, his
tongue plundering the soft interior of her mouth in a
way that was openly suggestive, his hands, pressing her
lower body against his, bringing her startlingly alive to
the hard reality of his arousal.

She uttered a small sound against his mouth, her
breathing shallow beneath the hard irregularity of his.
And suddenly her resistance seemed to snap and she was
submitting to his kiss—returning it—unable to deny any
longer that what she wanted was to be in this man's arms,
her own going up around his neck as she strained towards him in urgent, hungry response.

'Oh, hell...Fern!' His raggedly breathed words convinced her of the strength of her surprising effect on
him, and she breathed a soft sigh of pleasure as his lips
left hers to taste the smooth inviting satin of her throat.

'Oh, please, please...' She was lost to reality, sensation meeting sensation as her hands slid uninhibited
over the pristine silk of his shirt, revelling in the heavy
thunder of his heart, the heat of his body, his very intimate scent, her fingers finding their way beneath the
partially buttoned shirt to meet the velvet warmth of his
skin, the crisp texture of body hair beneath the strong,
sinewy column of his throat. Through the heat of desire
she felt the cool breeze on her skin, heard it rustling
through the leaves where the night creatures sang their
song regardless—unseen, impartial witnesses to Connor's
passion and her own abandoned response.

'I want you, Fern.' She heard him sigh his need
through a heady torture of sweet ecstasy, because he had

pushed aside the cross-over fabric of her thin top and was caressing the full, soft mound of her breast, and she gave a soft sigh as the sensitive peak blossomed in aching sweetness beneath his warm, well-practised hands. 'I'm perpetually haunted by the memory of you lying half naked in my bed. I want you there again, Fern, but I shan't abandon you the way Greg did. I'll be there, my love, until you're begging me to leave, and only then if I'm ready to. By the time I've finished with you, little Jezebel, Greg Peters and every other man will have ceased to exist.'

His ragged castigation brought her back to reality, and to exactly what it was he was trying to do. Breathless and dishevelled, she pulled violently away from him, seeing through an already rampant remorse the desire that rode him, the dark emotion in his face, though his voice when he spoke sounded surprisingly cool and detached.

'Well?' A black eyebrow arched in cold, derisive query. 'What is it to be? Your room or mine?'

She didn't stay to give him the satisfaction of an answer, pushing past him and running up the steps, her only aim to get away from him, her cheeks burning with humiliation. She'd played right into his hands, she scolded herself silently, ashamed of the way she had so easily responded to him, seeing plainly now his reason for bringing her to Bermuda. Not just, as he clearly assumed, to remove temptation from Greg, but, more insidiously, to try and stop her breaking up his friend's marriage by using that lethal animal magnetism of his to lure her into his own bed!

Well, he wouldn't succeed! she determined, brushing at her humiliated, angry tears. But she knew a deflated feeling too, as she turned back to the hotel—a deep and aching emptiness she didn't even want to understand.

* * *

The others were already in Reception talking to Connor when Fern came downstairs the following day, and, feeling his gaze resting on her with disconcerting intentness, she offered him only the remnants of her smile in response to his cool, 'Good morning,' careful not to meet his eyes.

'Well?' she said brightly, wrestling with the shameful memory of her behaviour with him the previous night, and, keeping her attention on Jenny—casually dressed, like herself, in blouse and shorts—and Tony, weighed down with cameras and cases, she enquired, 'Are we ready to go?'

The morning was beautiful, still and already surprisingly hot as they stepped out of the hotel, but as they came through the almond trees to the steps above the wharf mental images of what had happened down there last night trespassed with such shocking clarity on Fern's senses that an uncomfortable heat stole over her which had nothing to do with the sun.

'Something troubling you, Fern?' With innate courtesy, Connor stood aside for her to precede him down the steps after the other two, those shrewd eyes clearly aware of the reason for her colour-burned cheeks.

'No. Should there be?' she enquired, with a forced smile in his direction, her pulses responding to the magnificent maleness of him in the light cotton shirt and the pale, hip-hugging Bermudas. 'I'm looking forward to starting work, aren't you?'

He didn't answer, only with a quirk of lips that silently assured her he wasn't fooled.

Apart from that he made no further reference to that shaming interlude between them only hours before, for which Fern was immensely relieved. She had a job to do, and she couldn't do it to the best of her ability if disturbing and totally foolhardy aspects of her private life were allowed to intrude. Which was probably

Connor's own clever thinking, she deduced, because she didn't doubt that, in different circumstances, he would probably have enjoyed watching her squirm. Even so, she was glad when the launch Jenny had organised was carrying them away from the wharf, north-westward to the bay where Connor's company yacht was anchored.

A sleek white monster of a craft, the *Host* had Jenny and Tony openly expressing appreciation over Fern's own quiet wonderment as they stepped on to the warm, polished teak of the deck.

'I take it you're not impressed.' Connor was beside her, his lips mocking as the buzz of the retreating launch reverberated back across the wide bay.

'Oh, very.' Fern's hands tightened on the shining chrome of the rail, an uneasy awareness creeping through her. He'd still made no mention of the previous night, and she could only assume that he'd chosen to forget it, trying to do the same as her eyes took in the imposing rigging and unhoisted sails—since they were shooting on her moorings today—the sheer opulence of the yacht a silent tribute to a man who had made it, and made it big. 'Who wouldn't be?' she admitted, looking guardedly up into those impenetrable features, feeling the tug of something strong and undeniable in the sudden tightening of her stomach. 'You've certainly got it right! What company would dream of relinquishing their account with you when you go to these lengths to retain customer goodwill?'

A muscle pulled in his cheek as he leaned on the rail, his profile beautifully austere in its regard of other small craft moored on the sparkling blue water.

'People aren't really that naïve,' he said. 'If service and goods satisfaction aren't met then you can kiss goodbye to the custom—regardless of what little perks you might be planning to throw in as an added incentive. Apart from which, consumer goodwill is only a small part of the role the *Host* was built to play.'

'Well, naturally,' she said, feeling distinctly as though that remark about naïveté had been directed at her. And, finding it necessary suddenly that he should respect her intelligence, if not her morals, she went on to expand, 'Your company's continued business with mine is a prime example. It wouldn't matter how good a job I did here if the future service we gave you didn't come up to scratch.'

Connor's mouth pulled one side. 'Which it will, I'm sure, if what I've seen of your work so far is anything to go by.' He seemed to tower above her as he moved to lean back against the chrome, studying her with such intense interest that she felt each little pulse-point start to throb. 'Where did you develop those artistic skills, Fern, or are they entirely inborn?'

'Partly, I suppose.' She laughed a little nervously, tension riding her. 'Though I think a two-year course at art college helped!'

'So talent, plus tuition, equals genius!'

Now he was really laughing at her, she thought, even if that smile did add a breath-catching charm to that lethal virility of his. And before she could say anything he was jerking his chin deckwards and saying, 'Would you like to see below?'

She nodded, wondering if the others would be joining them as well, but he didn't suggest it, and, with a tightening in her throat, she obeyed his courteous gesture and went ahead of him, leaving the photographer trying out various camera angles and Jenny simply enjoying the view.

Below, soft furnishings added luxury to shining brass and the warm richness of polished mahogany, both the spacious saloon and cabins embracing a purity of affluence affordable only by the mega-rich.

'I approve,' Fern told Connor on a quavering note, feeling his strong physical presence dominating in the private, cushioned luxury of the saloon. 'You must think a lot of the people who work for you—keeping something like this for the occasional boost to their morale!'

'They do a good job,' he said succinctly. 'They deserve something more besides just a regular pay-cheque at the end of the month. But I didn't have it built solely to woo customers and my senior management.'

Of course, he would use it for his own enjoyment, she realised, imagining him leaning against the rail as he was doing earlier, with the wind blowing through the rich ebony of his hair. A man in control of his own destiny. Not a slave to riches as Ross Walker was, but master of them, because, unlike Ross, he knew—Franklin had conveyed to her only that week—what it was to be born without. And of course he would bring his women here...

Simultaneously their eyes met, and suddenly the air seemed to be charged with sizzling currents. Fern touched her tongue to her lips, finding the saloon suddenly too confining, much too intimate. But then the buzz of a speedboat and shrieks of feminine laughter announced the arrival of Ross, over half an hour late, with four bikini-clad beauties, one of whom was Madree.

'Damn the man! He never could learn to separate business from pleasure,' she heard Connor swear under his breath as he glanced through the small oblong window, though from what he had been saying before that party the other night she'd imagined he would normally indulge the younger man's shortcomings. So why did she have the distinct impression that it was somehow because of her that he'd taken this attitude now?

'Hi, baby.' As they came back on deck, Madree's smile excluded everyone but Connor as he gallantly helped her aboard, and Fern pretended not to notice the way the model stepped deliberately into his arms, hands coming to rest familiarly against his shoulders, her dark skin contrasting perfectly with the pale cotton of his shirt.

Some friend! she thought, absently aware of the speedboat whisking the superfluous girls away, noticing how slender and feminine Madree looked against Connor's intense masculinity, and so beautiful that she couldn't help wondering how the woman Franklin had termed 'the lovely lady in his life' would compare, as she said with forced brightness, 'Right. Shall we get started?'

Her eagerness concealed a twist of sharp, indefinable emotion which she didn't care to question, but which produced a pouting objection from Madree.

'My, she's keen, isn't she, Connor? Is she always such a slavedriver?' she queried, looking at Fern as though she was something that had slithered up out of the deep.

Connor clearly didn't consider her question worthy of an answer, for which Fern was grateful to him as, with practised cordiality, he acquainted her with the model.

'Welcome to the assignment, Madree,' Fern greeted politely with a firm handshake that seemed to take the other girl rather by surprise. 'I'm sorry if things are moving too quickly for you, but time, I'm afraid, is money, and, as I'm answerable to my client for every penny I spend, I can't imagine he'd be very pleased if I began by wasting his time.'

The model looked about to say something in retaliation, clearly irked at being issued instructions by someone she probably considered younger than herself, Fern thought with a long-suffering sigh, surprised to hear Connor suddenly backing her.

'Do as she says, Madree.' The deep male voice brooked no argument, so that the girl uttered a sultry little laugh, her perfect white teeth complementing the glossy lips that matched her red bikini as she looked up at Connor in a way that seemed to wish the others would disappear.

'Well, if *you're* giving the orders, darling...'

It was, Fern decided waspishly, an overt declaration of enslavement by Madree to the man's devastating sexuality, as well as one of sole claim, as she reached up on tiptoe to press her lips against that thrusting jaw.

So what did she care? she asked herself, with an unexpected resurgence of that sick, jealous emotion, a feeling that wasn't helped, as the morning wore on, by the others' silent yet patent agreement with Madree that they were under Connor's command, to the point that Fern began to feel her position being undermined.

The last straw came during the setting up of a shot they were taking of Ross—complete with ALI's latest wet-suit, cylinders and a jewelled dagger from one of his luckier dives—and the photographer called Connor over for his opinion on the composition. It was something that had already been agreed between Fern and Tony from the graphics her team had supplied, and she was incensed to hear Connor saying, 'I know what she wanted, but it clearly isn't going to work.'

And his idea would! she fumed, waiting until he'd supplied his obviously very valued suggestions to Tony before she decided to state her mind.

'If you don't need my services, why don't you say so?' she confronted him with when they were standing some distance away from the others. He was an important client, after all, and it was beyond her integrity to challenge him in front of anyone else. 'If I remember correctly, I'm only here because you forced me to be. I didn't want to come,' she reminded him, her tension showing in her face as she slid a hand under her hair at the nape of her neck, massaging the tight muscles. 'However, if you think you can do my job better than I can, change everything we agreed, then I might as well just not be here,' she expostulated. It was just adding insult to injury, that was all!

Against the boat the water lapped gently, stirring the luxurious craft, while the chink-chink of something metallic on the rigging was drowned beneath a burst of sudden laughter from the others.

'I was hoping we could work together,' said Connor, the strained conciliation in the strongly defined features overridden by a sighed impatience with her which prompted her impetuous reply.

'Well, obviously we can't!'

For a moment he stood facing her, hands on his hips, his countenance taking on decidedly tougher lines before he said quietly, 'Grow up, Fern,' and strode away from her with a tight-lipped grimness as though he had better things to do than stay and argue with her.

Feeling thoroughly chastened, Fern took a deep breath. Was she being childish? she asked herself. She didn't think so, even though she might rather have taken the defensive over some of the suggestions he had made earlier, she reflected, the truth goading her.

Now the model had gone below deck, complaining, rather needlessly, Fern felt, that she had had too much sun and would have to lie down. Consequently, feeling rather battle-weary herself, and with work at a standstill for a while, she was pleased when the treasure-hunter invited her to join him in a swim.

Tanned and smooth-skinned, he had peeled off the restricting wet-suit, and he gave a low whistle as Fern slipped off her blouse and shorts.

'That's some swimsuit, sugar!'

Cut high in the leg, with a cut-away waist, the slinky black garment seemed to expose more than she remembered it doing in the shop back in England, and suddenly she felt extremely self-conscious, not because of Ross's appreciative scrutiny, but because Connor was just coming up from below and had stopped dead, that dark, brooding gaze seeming to strip every last thread of the scanty swimsuit from her body.

Looking up at Ross, she gave a trembling little laugh. 'Well, I knew I'd be meeting you,' she told him, loud enough for Connor to hear, knowing she was being unfair to Ross by leading him on. But she was determined to let Connor see that she wasn't interested in him, she justified silently to herself, refusing to give air-space to the thought that it was because he'd just spent some time below deck with Madree. Nevertheless, those glowering features sent a small shiver down her spine as she plunged after Ross into the sea.

The water was surprisingly warm, and, coming up for air, Fern struck out towards the treasure-hunter, who was treading water several yards away.

'We aren't likely to meet any sharks, are we?' she laughed tensely, trying to put Connor McManus out of her mind.

'Don't worry, you're perfectly safe,' Ross smiled. 'The coral reefs round these islands tend to keep those hungry little monsters out. But outside the barrier you've got to treat those creatures with respect—and anything else that might be lurking down there.'

'Oh, don't!' Fern shuddered laughingly, following his example now and treading water. 'If you've had any close encounters I don't want to know about them just at the moment, thank you!'

'Sorry to disappoint you.' Ross moved, floating effortlessly on his back, while another deep splash told Fern that someone else was also taking the plunge. Resolutely, however, she didn't turn around. 'The only worrying moments I've had were over my oxygen equipment failing when I was diving off the west coast of the States some years back. Fortunately Connor was with me that day and came to the rescue, or I might have wound up in a watery grave. When we got back on the boat the first thing he said was that it wouldn't have happened if the equipment I'd been wearing had been ALI's!'

'Typical!' grimaced Fern, ignoring an absurd tingle of admiration in learning that Connor was experienced enough a diver to be able to extend help to a seasoned professional like Ross Walker.

'That's Connor,' he drawled, his blue gaze roving over her as tangibly as the sun she could feel on her back and shoulders as she began a leisurely breast-stroke around him. 'Always in control. Never taking risks unless they're calculated and ninety-nine per cent certain, and always so darn infuriatingly right—but one of the best, nevertheless. I met him at a diving club in the States, and even ten years ago we could all see he was destined for great things. Only he could produce the innovative wet-suit that every other manufacturer would automatically want to copy—plus putting ALI at the top of the leading marine retailers in the world!'

Yes, but he was that type of man, Fern acknowledged silently in spite of herself, and couldn't account for the little tremor in her voice as she responded lightly, 'Hero-worship, Ross?'

He made a playful grab for her, but she was too quick for him, disappearing under the water and swimming shorewards with a proficiency acquired from a father who had taught her to swim even before she could properly walk.

Within her depth, she let her feet touch the cool, sandy bottom, the water lapping gently above her breasts. Ahead, mangroves formed a green backdrop for the wide, sloping arc of amber sand where the turquoise water broke in lazy ripples along its edge. A handful of people were basking on the beach, bodies tanned,

gleaming with oil, and, about to swim in, Fern dropped
a glance to the water, something caught her eye, and she
froze, her breath a horrified gasp.

CHAPTER SIX

NOT a yard away, the gelatinous blue mass of a Portuguese man-of-war—the worst kind of jellyfish—bobbed on the placid surface, but beneath it, Fern knew, were lethal tentacles that could produce a dangerous, even deadly, sting.

Her mouth dry, she backed cautiously away, forgetting in her fear that she was almost out of her depth, and she stumbled, the water washing over her so that she floundered wildly for a few seconds, surfacing with a small, choked cry of alarm.

Suddenly strong arms were lifting her up out of the water, wading with powerful, effortless strides towards the beach, brief moments when she knew the shattering contact of hair-roughened flesh against her own before she was placed carefully down on to the sun-warmed sand.

'For goodness' sake, Fern, say something! Did it sting you?' Connor's voice was urgent and concerned.

'No, I...' She was trembling, but more from being rescued like that by those capable arms than from any possible encounter with the jellyfish. 'No, I don't think so,' she finished shakily, sitting up and pulling her wet hair out of her face.

'What do you mean, you don't think so?' Was that relief in his voice? she wondered, amazed, watching the water dripping off his hair and running through that dark matted triangle of hair that tapered down into a thin line and disappeared beneath dark red trunks. 'If you'd been stung you'd know it all right!' he assured her, and almost angrily, 'Don't you ever scare the life out of me like that again!'

So he *had* been concerned! 'I didn't know you were so worried about me,' she breathed, unable to stem the reckless elation that knowledge produced.

From under her lashes she noticed the hard compression of his lips as he stretched out beside her, leaning back on his elbows, a disconcerting statement of masculine fitness and virility. 'Of course I was bloody well worried!' he rasped, that lean abdomen tautening with controlled emotion. 'I feel responsible for you, that's why.' Well, what else? she thought, strangely deflated, as he went on, 'I should have warned you about those jellies before you swam off like that on your own— and Ross should have had more common sense than to let you do it.'

'It wasn't his fault,' she returned in defence of the treasure-hunter, whose fair head she could see bobbing above the blue water way out beyond the *Host* and the other small boats in the glittering bay. 'I should just have been more wary.' After all, she'd seen enough signs around warning bathers to be aware of jellyfish. 'Is it a common occurrence, meeting one of those things?' she asked with an involuntary shudder.

As though sensitive to it, Connor gave her a half-smile, his anger dissipating now. 'No, believe it or not, it's surprisingly rare,' he reassured her against the hum of light traffic on the narrow road beyond the mangrove trees. 'It's only usually after a storm that they get washed in. You were just unfortunate finding one on your first time in the water.'

Unfortunate? It could have been disastrous if he hadn't come along when he had! At the very least she could have been in a great deal of discomfort now, she thought, shuddering again, and, grateful to him, she murmured, 'Thanks...for rescuing me, I mean. I wouldn't have panicked like that, but I was in deeper water than I thought.' She suddenly felt the need to convey all this, and instantly regretted it when it prompted him to respond softly,

'Seems to be a habit of yours, doesn't it?' He was sitting up with his arms resting on his drawn-up knees, his gaze so darkly censuring that Fern sucked her lips and looked away, stiffening as he went on, 'Isn't it enough that you're ruining Greg's marriage, without fooling around with every other man besides?'

He was referring to her behaviour with Ross—and himself last night. As well he might! she thought, cringing at how her morals must appear to him, although annoyance at his own lack of them had her retorting heedlessly, 'I'd hardly call going for a swim with someone fooling around! Not like some I could mention who spend half the morning practising their bedside manner with my staff!'

'Hardly half the morning,' drawled Connor in response to her heated exaggeration, 'and even if it were...' his voice breathed cool authority ' . . . I think that would be my prerogative, Fern, don't you?'

Because he was paying the bill—that was what he was saying, she realised, colouring from the chastening subtlety of his reminder.

'What's wrong, darling—jealous?' he taunted softly, his smile coolly perceptive, because, heaven help her, she was!

'Of course not!' she snapped, praying he wouldn't guess, struggling for composure as she stared seawards.

A little way along the beach someone coughed—a middle-aged woman with a man, paddling at the water's edge, and, watching them, suddenly Fern flinched, sucking in her breath as Connor placed an unexpected hand upon her shoulder. 'You're burning,' he remarked in cool, practical tones. 'Don't you think you'd better move into the shade?'

She knew she should, but the warm contact of his fingers had immobilised her, and she murmured tremulously, 'No, I'm all right,' pulling away from that disturbing contact with him.

'You seem it,' he observed drily. She could feel his eyes studying her tense profile as she watched a kiskadee that had just taken off from one of the mangrove bushes behind them, a splash of yellow against the cloudless blue of the sky. 'Last night you didn't seem quite so...eager to avoid my touch.'

The reminder scorched Fern's cheeks with colour. 'Last night I'd had too much to drink!' she lied, springing up, only to be caught by hard, determined fingers around her wrist, pulling her back so that she landed in an undignified heap across his lap.

'Like hell!' Above the drumming of her heart she caught his softly laughed expletive, felt the sensuous brush of his body hair against her skin. 'Out of character though it would seem, you've been very adept at keeping your consumption to the barest minimum since you've been here—and last night was no exception. That response was totally uninfluenced by alcohol, Fern, and you know it,' he stated bluntly, shocking her into realising how closely he had been observing her. 'So why lie about it? You wanted my kisses, just as you're begging for them now—because God knows I want you to have them, little sea-nymph.'

As he pulled her hard against him she had no strength, no desire, to deny it, her head falling back against his arm, lips parting in willing surrender to the bitter-sweet domination of his. She could taste the sea-salt on his skin, her nostrils distending from the scent of his warm, wet body, and her arm snaked up around his neck to draw him closer, driven by the need of him against every exposed inch of her trembling warmth.

There were people watching them, but she didn't care, sighing her agreement as Connor twisted her round beneath him on to the soft sand.

Mouth fused with his, her hands made a sensuous exploration over the muscled satin of his back, the effect she was having on him apparent in the way he caught his breath, and the sudden spasm of his body as her thumbs slid provocatively along those steel-caged ribs to the tense muscles of his waist and beyond.

'Just do that when we're alone and you'll answer for the consequences,' he breathed against her throat, his promise—his tenderness—so different from last night—exciting her, desire a knot of anguish in her loins as his lips strayed to her shoulder, the taut peaks of her breasts straining against the confining fabric of her swimsuit, aching for his caress.

If they were alone now he would make love to her. And she would be powerless to stop him, she realised hopelessly, so that suddenly it became imperative that he should know the truth about her and Greg—that he should believe her.

'Connor...'

'Hush...' His voice caressed like the soft ripple of waves along the shore, and a finger rested gently against her lips. 'Not now, darling. Don't spoil the moment,' he commanded softly, something in his voice prompting her to look up at him, lids heavy with desire. The wanting was evident in his eyes and the sensual flush beneath his skin, but there was a marked vulnerability in those usually controlled features that shocked her, brought her hand unwittingly to caress the rough texture of his cheek before his head dipped again, blotting out everything but the sweet ecstasy of his lips and his naked warmth pressing against her.

Sounds merged as one, the hum of traffic and the lapping water, and suddenly running footsteps, followed by the unexpected shock of sand on her face and giggling as little feet scampered away.

'The little...!' Immediately Connor was pushing himself up, a purposeful curve to his lips. 'I'll teach that little scamp...!'

In one fluid movement he was up and giving chase, and Fern laughed as he caught the giggling boy, who couldn't have been more than about six and, lifting him high above his head, ran with him to the water's edge, ostensibly to throw him into the sea. Shrieking with excitement, the child was obviously enjoying this game, Fern realised, still laughing as Connor deposited the boy into the middle of a sand-castle and stuck a flag in his hair.

'I hope that was a British flag,' she laughed as he ambled back to her, unable to take her eyes off the lithe perfection of that beautifully proportioned physique. How one man could possess such dominating physical attraction, the sanctioning power of mind to control vast enterprises, and still be playful with children, filled her with reluctant awe.

'Actually it was a skull and crossbones,' he grinned.

Standing above her with those long-fingered hands splayed against his hips, he looked every bit the daunting, naked pirate who had just plundered a village and was savouring the rewards of ruthless victory, so that she said jestingly, 'Your true colours, Connor?' Her eyes were bright with teasing. 'Is the *Host* really a pirate's ship, a place to lure innocent maidens?'

Mockery gave a lazy curl to his lips. 'I've never had to resort to luring anyone,' he said softly, dropping to his haunches so that his gaze was level with hers, and in a voice impregnated with sensuality. 'Usually they'll follow me anywhere.'

Just as she had shown herself to be! Fern realised, reprimanding herself for the way she had so easily yielded to him again after vowing so resolutely last night that she wouldn't! All he wanted was her conquest, she thought woundedly, searching for something to say to salve her pride, but any retort was curbed by Madree coming up the beach, jealousy dripping from her like the water from her bikini, as she complained to Fern, 'If you aren't going to use me again today, I might just as well not be here.' And with that alluring pout at Connor, 'I waited for you, darling, but you didn't come back down. I wouldn't have minded too much, but you *did* promise.'

She didn't want to know this! Fern thought, catching Connor's soft curse as he got up, hauling her roughly to her feet.

'All right, Madree, I'm coming,' he said almost irritably, so that the Bermudan girl turned moodily back to the water.

'What's wrong? Wasn't she supposed to see us together?' Fern taunted, tugging free from him as Madree's graceful, dark limbs struck out again for the *Host*. 'I thought you said she was just a friend. Or are you scared she'll tell the others and word'll get back to someone else you obviously like to think has no claim on you?' she snapped, twirling away from him, but he came after her, his footsteps making angry impressions in the soft sand.

'Judging everyone else by your own standards, Fern?' His voice was cold and slicing. 'Are you always so ready to accuse every man of playing you at your own game?'

No, just you! her heart clamoured, stabbed by his continuing contempt for her, and, ignoring his shout, she tore away from him, nursing a cold desolation that refused to be eased even by the warm blue ocean as she cut tempestuously through the water, back to the boat.

*   *   *

Fortunately, over the next couple of days, the pressure of work and the presence of the others was enough to prevent any enforced intimacy between them. Fortunately, too, Madree wasn't needed the day they did the underwater photography, and, though Fern told herself she was only relieved because she simply didn't get on with the model, she knew that it wasn't the true reason, although, by the same token, she didn't dare to consider what the real reason might be.

They were working off the reefs on the South Shore, using the convenient location of a sunken wreck that Ross had previously explored, and in the hired launch, with Jenny helping Ross and the Hamilton photographer on with their oxygen tanks, Fern couldn't prevent a sudden flutter in her stomach, as she noticed the way the black wet-suit clung to Connor's muscular body as she helped him fasten his own tank in position.

'Take care, Connor.' It was out before she could stop it as Ross and the photographer dropped simultaneously over the side. And when a black eyebrow lifted in derisive query, she added quickly, 'After all, you're our biggest client. Lose you and the company could lose one hell of an account!'

'What else?' he accepted drily, turning round to allow himself to fall easily into the blue water with an echoing splash after the other two.

It seemed an eternity before anyone surfaced, and then it was only Connor, bringing the two girls anxiously to the side of the boat as he climbed in, allowing them to assist him off with his tank.

'Don't look so worried,' he advised, his smile allaying any suspicions and fears they might have had that something had gone wrong. 'The other two are still down there taking photos, but for anyone who likes marine life all you need to do is skim the surface to get a good enough picture of what it's like down there.' And to Fern, 'Get a snorkel and some goggles and come on in.'

She didn't need to be invited twice. She was already wearing her swimsuit under her sundress, and moments later she knew a thrill from more than just the sheer ecstasy of the warm ocean as she followed Connor back in.

The underwater world presented a spectacle of colour that was breathtaking in its beauty. Small striped fish, yellow and black, darted in and out of the filigreed structure of the coral. A shoal turned, like delicate, darting strands of silver where the sun's rays penetrated the crystal-clear water. Then the sudden startling blue of a parrot-fish, nosing into crevices where other, iridescent specimens sought food among the living splendour of the reef.

'It's beautiful!' she gasped, her face above water again, goggles and mouthpiece pushed aside so that she could talk to Connor. 'I just wish I could take some of those little specimens back home for my tank. Do you think I could smuggle some back on the plane?' she joked.

'I don't see why not—as long as their passports are in order,' he drawled, treading water, and with such a mischievous slant to that sensual mouth that, impetuously, she splashed him—hard—right in the face, darting laughingly away from him before he could catch her.

When she turned with a gentle side-stroke, he was nowhere to be seen. There was only the launch, some distance away, with its lifelines hanging over the side, and occasionally she grasped the muted tones of Jenny and the skipper above the continuous boiling surf breaking over the reef.

Everything appeared ominously quiet, like the lull before a storm. And then she shrieked as a hand grabbed her ankle, pulling her under, and she felt Connor's arm lock around her, clasping her to him as he surfaced with

her, laughing as she coughed and spluttered and beat at
him in trembling, amiable protest.

'I thought that was what you wanted—my attention.
Isn't that why all little girls misbehave?'

Yes, and he knew just how to deal with them! Fern
thought with a sharp *frisson*, feeling the ripple of muscle
beneath the smooth rubber of his wet-suit and the supple
power of the thighs that were entangling with hers.

'Even you aren't that clever!' she laughed, with a
nervous, impish teasing, because he was needing his other
arm and both legs to keep the pair of them afloat. And
as a diversion from the fierce thrust of pleasure jabbing
at her loins, she asked seriously, 'Is there really still a
fortune, as Ross keeps telling me, undiscovered down
there under these waters?'

She wasn't sure why his body seemed to tense beneath
the warm buoyancy of the water. 'Depends what you
mean by a fortune,' he said curtly, releasing her. Then
he took a dive, his long, lithe body propelling away from
her with a beauty all its own, and feeling oddly chas-
tised, as well as concerned about burning, Fern decided
to call it a day.

She had a towel round her shoulders when he climbed
back into the launch and was unaware of how intently
she was watching him as he peeled his wet suit from that
tanned, sinewy body—until he gave her such a knowing
smile that she blushed profusely and feigned a sudden
interest in Jenny, who was sitting writing a postcard to
her mother.

'Here,' he said, thrusting a cold, wet object into her
hand. 'Ross might not be totally in agreement with me,
but here's one of the real riches of the deep.'

Fern looked at the small piece of coral, turning the
ivory structure over in her hands, admiring its
honeycomb patterning as if it were a priceless jewel. Had
he got it especially for her? she wondered, feeling a con-

striction in her throat. She looked up to thank him, but he had already walked away across to the helm to talk to the skipper.

If she had thought he was softening towards her because of that incident, Fern still found that their working relationship continued to bring moments of strain. Like the morning they were photographing the new speedboat, designed by ALI's American subsidiary, and which was to occupy a whole page in the new brochure. Madree had posed for the stills—looking beautiful, if not wholly convincing, Fern thought, swiftly rebuking herself for her unkind speculation—at the wheel.

Now, though, from the wharf, while guests in the outdoor restaurant looked casually on, they started shooting the vessel in action with the water-skiing scenes and, pleased with the way things were going, Fern breathed an exasperated sigh as Connor directed an order to her photographer.

'Hold it a few minutes, Tony!'

'You're the boss.'

Needled by the other man's compliant statement, Fern bit her tongue. Her silent indignation, however, didn't go unnoticed, because drily, over the throaty growl of the speedboat slicing across the Sound, Connor was advising, 'I wouldn't let Fern hear you say that, if I were you. It could be more than your life's worth.'

He was testing her, she could see it in his eyes—a deliberate snide remark that unfortunately had her retorting, 'No, it's all right!' Both pique and impatience coloured her voice now. 'Feel free to take over if——'

'I don't want to take over anything,' he was interrupting with sudden hard assurance. 'Merely to make a suggestion. Take a look at that parakite over there.' Rather roughly, regardless of the others watching, he pulled her in front of him to the camera on the tripod, his impatience with her evident in the firm clamp of his hands. 'As Madree came past it just now her whole body was haloed in red. If you could catch the two together...' He went on to explain what he had in mind, that deep voice warm and enthusiastic, adding in conclusion, 'If you'll work with me instead of against me for a change, it could provide an added bonus to an already brilliant concept.'

Fern looked thoughtful, considering what he was suggesting, while trying to ignore his nearness, the pulsing warmth emanating from him.

He was right, she thought, peering through the lens, knowing a heart-lifting pleasure from his remark that her idea was brilliant. But his added something extra ...

'OK, Madree, you'll have to do it again!' she called out eagerly as the boat stopped, broadside, engine burring, beside the wharf. 'I want you to take this thing up as close as you can to that boat out there and then sweep round...' Avidly she went on, unaware of Connor watching her with a cool, complacent smile as she issued her instructions to the man at the wheel. Then, as the boat growled away, she began conferring with Tony over things like minimisation of glare from the water, other background craft, and the general composition. 'Right! Now, shoot!'

Unfortunately the first shots failed as another speedboat came unexpectedly into their field of vision, and then the parakite moved, too high to be of any use to them. Eventually it was a question of a few large cocktails, and the parakiters were more than pleased to assist in achieving the desired effect, and as the last shots were being taken Fern turned to Connor with, 'That's great!' Her face was aglow with satisfaction—and gratitude. 'Thanks,' she murmured rather humbly, waiting for him to make some smug comment, knowing she'd have deserved it if he had.

But he didn't, merely dipping his head with a softly drawled, 'Don't mention it,' which only had her unwillingly warming to him, respecting him more.

That particular instance seemed to lift a lot of the tension out of their professional relationship, so that working with him actually became fun. However, this new working rapport only served to heighten the already devastating sexual tension between them, so that, when Connor invited her to go sailing with him one afternoon, like the coward she felt she was, she declined.

'I'm sorry, but I've made arrangements...' She watched him set her portfolios of drawings and paperwork he'd helped carry to her room down on to the chest beneath the window, noticed the play of muscle beneath the soft T-shirt he was wearing, and that inevitable clutch of desire gripped at her loins.

'Can't you break them?'

He was smiling as he came over to her where she was standing near the bed, the gentle touch of his hands on her shoulders, his very nearness, causing every nerve to sing with a wild excitement.

'I can't,' she said lamely, wishing she hadn't already agreed to let Ross show her the Maritime Museum— wishing she had the courage to involve herself in the sort of relationship she knew Connor would expect from her. But she couldn't—not without getting hurt. And swallowing, in a more tentative voice, 'I—I promised Ross...'

'I might have guessed.' She winced from the sudden bruising pressure of his grip as grooves lined his face from that careless declaration. 'Me. Greg. Ross. It doesn't matter who it is as long as it's wearing trousers, does it?' Connor rasped scornfully, his mouth twisting with his contemptuous survey of her small, despairing features. 'Maybe you'd prefer it if I just went ahead and took what you seem so ready to offer any man who comes within a yard of you? Perhaps you'd prefer to spend the afternoon with me here, Fern—is that it? Is that how you fit us all in to your busy schedule—by dispensing with preliminaries!'

'No!' He was forcing her towards the bed, his intention as glaring as his anger, only that frantic negation on her part stopping him from carrying it out. 'I know how it looks, but it isn't like that!' she stressed, frightened by his implacable mood. She was only going to the museum with Ross because he'd found out that she hadn't yet seen it, and she'd only agreed to go with him then because he'd said some of his own finds were being exhibited—because she'd thought it would be rude to refuse. 'I'm not——'

'That's debatable!' He'd put his own interpretation on what she had been going to say, pushing her from him so forcibly that she almost fell back on to the bed. 'I don't give a damn what you do with your boyfriend, but let me make myself understood. We've been invited to the Breakers tonight, and that means *all* the team— including you. Williams is a valued customer of mine and he's already flying ALI's flag among his friends and other big businessmen on this island—so for the sake of my company's name you'll show your good manners in respect of his hospitality and dine at his hotel. Do I make myself clear?'

'And what if I decide not to?' Fern tossed back in angry contest, deliberately needling him, because protocol would never have let her refuse the hotelier's kind invitation.

Even so, the warning behind Connor's softly breathed, 'Be there,' before he slammed out of the room, had her wondering shudderingly at the outcome if she dared to cross that inexorable masculinity.

She wasn't sure if that was when her headache started, but by the time Ross picked her up in a flashy, low-slung cabriolet, it had already taken a hold. Consequently, her

enjoyment of the island's dockyard, with its museum
and arts centre and its fortress—built by convicts in the
last century to protect the island's shipbuilding area—
was impaired, and with Ross's continual commentary
on the ancient gold exhibits and the wrecks they had
come from, her brain felt like a maritime history book
that had been put through the blender by the time they
started their journey back.

'You know, you're a very beautiful girl.' He had pulled
into a layby—ostensibly for them to drink in the view
of a pink-gold bay, deserted save for a couple of bobbing
figures snorkelling in the warm blue ocean—and Fern's
head throbbed as she became aware of the arm suddenly
snaking across the back of her seat. 'Beautiful, intelligent—and with the most captivating eyes I've ever seen.'

'Oh, Ross!' Tensely she laughed, flushed from his ef-
fusive compliments and the gaze that swept down over
her pale blue suntop and shorts.

'Like amber gems!' he continued to extol, the chink
of metal as he took something from the glove com-
partment drawing a small gasp from her.

It was a thick-set amber stone on a chunky gold
chain—like the type of fashion jewellery she usually
avoided as too gaudy and artificial-looking, except that
this was obviously one of his lucky 'finds' from the
deep—very old, very real and certainly anything but
cheap.

'No, Ross...!' Before she could stop him, he was
putting it around her neck, her efforts to prevent it
thwarted as she heard the clasp snap securely into place.

'No, Ross, please, I...' The necklace lay cold and
heavily against her skin and her hands went up to remove
it, but she couldn't unfasten the clasp.

'That's better,' he said, looking satisfied. 'I'm afraid
the fastener's faulty and not very easy to work.'

Was he telling her! 'Look...I hardly know you...' she started, wishing she hadn't when he smiled and moved closer.

'Then we're going to have to change all that, aren't we?' he said.

She stiffened as his blond head suddenly obstructed the view, her own throbbing. She really wasn't feeling up to handling a situation like this!

His kiss was gentle, yet surprisingly unmoving; the features of the man that floated before her closed lids were as dark as this man's were fair, the haunting vision piercing through her passivity with such a throb of longing that she only realised the folly of her dangerous imaginings when his arms tightened around her, his mouth suddenly hungry on hers.

'No, Ross, no! I don't want this...' Shamefully, she pulled out of his arms. His breathing was heavy against the sound of the waves washing gently along the beach. Goodness, had her reckless imagination led him into thinking he was arousing her? 'I'm sorry, I didn't mean to give you the wrong impression.' Desperately she groped for an excuse for her mindless behaviour, hands pressed against his gaily-printed T-shirt, restraining him from kissing her again. 'I wasn't thinking...'

'No?' A blond eyebrow shot upwards. 'You didn't seem to be doing too badly.' He frowned when she held him off as he tried to clasp her to him again. 'What exactly where you thinking of?' The Aussie-American tones were strung with hard scepticism. 'Connor McManus, perhaps?' And when his shrewdness drew a startled look from her, 'Is that why you came out with me today? To make him jealous?'

'No!' Of course she hadn't. Had she? Surely she wasn't so crazily affected by the man that she would risk the type of reaction she had unconsciously provoked this afternoon? 'I came out with you...well, because I like you,' she attempted to explain judiciously, knowing she wasn't being wholly truthful with herself or Ross. 'You wanted to show me some of the treasure you'd found, and I thought it would be nice, as I hadn't seen the museum——'

'Only when it comes down to the nitty-gritty, you'd rather be in bed with him.'

'No!'

Her emphatic denial caused both pale eyebrows to ascend now. 'Oh, come on! All he has to do is look at you and...well, you know what I mean.'

'No, I'm not sure I do, Ross,' Fern stated calmly, though her heart was thumping like the continuous hammer in her head. Was her susceptibility to his friend so obvious? 'All we have is a business relationship— nothing else,' she told him, none the less shakily—and started as he uttered a short guffaw of disbelief.

'Pull the other one, sugar plum,' she heard him saying, her eyes trained on the small pointed head of a lizard peeping out from the dark green fingers of a flowering yucca. 'Unless you just like leading men on, but I think I know enough about women to know you're not like that.'

Wasn't she? Numbly she stared at the yucca, doubting herself, delving into her mind to question her past behaviour with Greg. Had she ever led him to think that she was easy, even when she'd thought he was single? she wondered in retrospect, watching the lizard's quick movements as it turned, a flash of green and purple, before it disappeared again under the cloaking foliage, dark green against the brilliant blue backdrop of the sea. No, not once, she reassured herself. It was only Connor's accusations that were making her feel guilty, question her own morals. She had nothing to reproach herself for.

'You've got very little chance with him, you know.' With hooded eyes she saw Ross watching her as he sat back heavily in his seat. 'He was very deeply involved—well, engaged, in fact, to some dame once who went off with another guy—some married guy who told her he was going to divorce his wife. When he did, the girl didn't want to know. She wanted Connor to take her back, but I'm afraid Connor's not that stupid. He cut loose and has been very wary ever since. Even Madree can't tie him down, and goodness knows she's tried hard enough! I don't think he really trusts women that much any more.'

And that explained a lot, Fern thought, suddenly numb—suddenly understanding. No wonder he'd immediately jumped to all the wrong conclusions about her!

'You're wrong, Ross—about Connor and me,' she lied, fumbling with the clasp of the necklace again, feeling unbelievably dejected. But why? Surely she didn't like Connor in anything more than a physical sense, did she? 'Anyway, it was kind of you to offer me the necklace—but I really can't accept it.' Wearily she made another futile attempt to release it. 'Do you think you could undo it for me, please?'

'No, keep it on,' he said almost in appeal to her. 'While you're wearing it, it might just do something to endear me to you. When you leave Bermuda you can give it back if you like, but until then . . .' He shrugged, looking strangely like a man who had played all his chips and lost. 'Apart from which, it suits you much better than it suits me.'

Which was Ross, Fern decided when they were on the road again. Easy come, easy go. There were very few men who would part with something so valuable—and to a girl they scarcely knew; very few women, too, who wouldn't be tempted to let him, but as soon as it came off she would be giving it back to him—she was resolute about that.

CHAPTER SEVEN

FERN'S headache was blinding when Ross dropped her at the hotel, and as she stepped through the main doors Tony, dressed for tennis, was just coming out.

'Fancy a game with me and Jenny and that South American couple on the next table from ours?' he invited cordially, tapping the head of his racket.

'In this heat? You must be joking!' laughed Fern, because, although it was late into the afternoon, it was still extremely hot. 'Seriously, though, that would have been nice, but I don't really think a migraine's the thing to take on court.'

She took the photographer's sympathetic response with a reassurance that it wasn't too bad, and that it would be even better after a short siesta before they left for the South Shore.

It was. Getting up, she ran a bath, then tried in vain to remove the ostentatious piece of jewellery Ross had put around her neck, her gaze falling to the lump of coral on the dressing-table that Connor had surprised her with the other day.

Gently she fingered its hard, honeycomb surface, feeling something stir—swell—with frightening intensity inside her.

Odd, she considered, how the thing of no monetary value could affect her so much, while the other...

It had to come off, she thought, struggling with the necklace, eventually ringing Jenny's room number in exasperation to ask if she could help. Only the monotonous ring answered her. Consequently, she had to bathe with it on, but tried Jenny again afterwards, deducing that she'd probably caught the girl in the shower the first time, and that now she must have already gone down to wait for their taxi, because there was still no reply. As a result there was no alternative, she thought hopelessly, but to wear the infernal thing!

The hotel to which they had been invited occupied a cliff-high position overlooking the ocean, with terraced cottage accommodation rambling down the hillside to the beach.

Ross was getting out of his car as their taxi arrived. He came up to them, smiling approvingly at Fern—still wearing his gift—as he helped her out of the car, tossing a casual greeting at her two colleagues.

'Connor's already here,' he told her above the rumble of the ocean—unnecessarily, since Connor had told her himself earlier in the day that he had some business to discuss with the hotelier prior to dinner. She also knew that Madree, as part of the team, had been invited tonight, but still couldn't control a sudden, nerve-tautening emotion as Ross guided her to the cocktail lounge and she saw that the other girl had already arrived, any more than she could control the tightening in her stomach from the sight of Connor standing, breathtakingly elegant and sophisticated in a dark lounge suit, sharing a Martini and a joke with the lovely model.

'Ross—Fern.' His dark head inclined, the lights over the bar striking fire from the black hair. His smile, though, had faded and there was censure in the deep voice, detectable even above the strains of a calypso band across the cocktail lounge, and Fern knew why. The necklace! She was in her blue strapless dress, and had her hair pinned up—it stood out like the proverbial sore thumb. And if looks could wound, then those eyes, weighing up the price of that gold above the soft swell of her breasts, would have flayed the skin off her bones, she thought, with an involuntary shudder, though she knew Connor would have more tact than to quiz her about it in front of the others.

Fortunately, the dialogue during the meal was confined mainly to the progress of the assignment, but afterwards someone—Fern couldn't remember who—suggested they take their liqueurs out on to the terrace.

Darkness had fallen since they had first entered the restaurant, and now lanterns glowed on the hotel's pink walls and those of the little cottage quarters clinging to the hillside, along the balustrade upon which Fern moved over to lean, looking out at the crashing waves. Night had fused the ocean with the sky, where a waning moon hung like a slice of golden melon, but way below the beach was softly illuminated, the light, spilling over the waves and the pale pink crescent of sand, touching a rash of flowering yuccas rising upwards with the cliff.

'It's unbelievable!' Her voice was a breathless murmur, almost lost in the pounding of the ocean and the whistling of little reptiles in the foliage around the terrace.

'Isn't it just?' Chilling words that had her pivoting round, realising that it was Connor behind her, and not Ross as she had thought, and her skin prickled when she saw the way he was looking at the necklace, his eyes as hard and cold as its ostentatious amber stone. 'I see you had a very... rewarding afternoon.'

Those deep tones sought only to disparage, and angry colour crept up Fern's throat into her cheeks. 'I've had just about as much as I can stand of your insults, Connor!' Against the mingling sounds of the sea and the other conversations on the terrace, she stood facing that bitter contempt in him with spitting defiance. 'I didn't want this... necklace. I didn't ask for it—or *earn* it, as you're so distastefully insinuating! And I'm only wearing it now because I couldn't get the damn thing off! If you dislike me so much, why the hell don't you get yourself another art director, and perhaps we'll both be happier?' Her eyes, lifting to the dark, inscrutable planes of his face, burned with a wounded mutiny. What power, in heaven's name, did he have, that his remarks could hurt her this much? she threw at herself torturedly, knowing he would be well within his rights now if he rang Franklin Stone and had her taken off this assignment immediately, but she didn't care any more.

There was a tumultuous emotion in Connor; she could see that even beneath the shadows created by the soft lighting, and he started to say something, but the proprietor, a round little man with a ruddy face, came up to extend his compliments to her with the hope that she had enjoyed her meal, and she saw that fervid emotion banked down, cleverly camouflaged.

How easily he could handle his personal feelings, she thought enviously, that antagonism towards her well under control as he became the interested listener, the brilliant conversationalist, employing that unaffected charm and charisma that won him respect and esteem with everyone, she reluctantly had to accept.

'Do you two want to be alone, or can anyone join in?' The proprietor had drifted off, only to be replaced by an American couple. Fern recognised them as the pair she had seen on the beach at Mangrove Bay the day she had encountered that jellyfish, and she returned their rather inquisitive smiles, although beside her she heard Connor's swift intake of breath. 'I said to Wilbur when I saw you on that beach the other day that you had to be honeymooners at the very least, although now I don't know...'

The woman was glancing curiously at Ross, who was chatting to Jenny and Tony a few yards away, probably having seen her arrive with the treasure-hunter, while Connor had already been in the bar with the model, Fern surmised, feeling her colour rising. As Madree's would have been if she hadn't been beautifying herself in the powder-room! she couldn't help thinking almost cattily.

'My wife just believes in variety,' she heard Connor conveying outrageously to the woman for her audacity, and in normal circumstances would have found it funny if she hadn't detected that cold, clipped edge to his voice again as, mortifyingly, he went on, 'I haven't yet been able to convince her of the advantages of staying faithful to one man yet—but, believe me, I'm working on it!'

Fern couldn't believe he was saying this! And purely to shock the other two into backing off—which it did, very effectively! she noticed as, affronted, the couple moved quickly away.

'Was that really necessary?' she breathed, her pulses throbbing in traitorous awareness of that dark attraction he possessed, even through the hard determination she sensed in him to bring her eventually to heel.

'What's wrong, darling? I thought you had a sense of humour. Or have you traded that with your morals for anything in trousers you think might be able to give you a good time?'

His tongue meant to wound, which it did, and she made to retaliate with some futile, caustic retort which she had to bite back as the others came to join them at the rail.

'Migraine better?' asked Jenny with smiling concern, aware that her friend hadn't been in top form before they had arrived this evening.

'Yes…thanks,' answered Fern, and, though she wasn't looking at Connor, she felt herself the object of his concentrated regard.

'So that accounts for that insidious frailty about you tonight.' Surprisingly, concern lessened the severity in the chiselled contours of his face. 'Do you suffer very badly?'

It was as if they were alone, the censure behind that first, softly spoken remark producing a tension like a tightrope between them as she answered in a small, clipped voice, wishing Jenny hadn't brought it up, 'No, not really.'

'Oh, come off it!' the brunette persisted, to Fern's rising discomfiture. And to Connor, 'Nobody gets them like Fern!'

'I'm sure no one's interested in the boring details of my health, Jenny,' Fern laughed, embarrassed, but Jenny wasn't taking the hint.

'Just because you prefer to be a martyr and suffer in silence, those lucky enough not to don't understand what you have to put up with. Do you know, the last time she had a really bad one——'

'Jenny!' Mortified, her fingers tightening around her wine glass, Fern attempted to curb the other girl's well-meaning spiel, but in heart-sinking dismay she heard the pretty brunette carrying on '—she was in a friend's apartment and felt so bad she had to go to bed, and the person who owned the place came back in the middle of the night, found her being ill, and accused her of having too much to drink, when she hadn't touched a drop!'

Everyone else's laughing amazement was lost on Fern as her eyes clashed reproachfully with Connor's. Because she had been feeling so dreadful, she had confided in Jenny about that incident when she hadn't known who he was, and then, when she'd found out, she had felt too embarrassed to tell her friend that it had been their most prestigious client. Now she saw those thick brows come together, his eyes burning with a shocked clarity as, absently, she caught Tony's dry, astonished, 'What a nerve! I hope you thumped him one.'

There was a gauntness to her features as she held Connor's hard, interrogative gaze and said with tight-lipped acidity, 'No, but I felt like it.'

She could feel the intensity of his anger flicking across her raw nerves; sensed, too, that everyone could feel the electricity sizzling in the air from the sudden awkward silence that had fallen on the group, and then Jenny's dawning, awkward, 'Oh, God! Gosh, I'm sorry...'

Burning with remorse over her own lack of restraint, Fern mechanically dumped her glass down on a table nearby and pulled out of the little circle without another word, shamefully conscious of the shocked surprise on the faces of her two colleagues before that deep voice ripped across the distance she had put between them with angry impatience.

'Fern!'

If anyone had been in any doubt, then they all knew now, she thought despairingly, her quickening steps bringing her off the terrace to the forecourt, busy with taxis and people arriving and leaving. Wanting only to be alone, she turned down some steps in front of the first of the pink cottages and came on to a patio where soft lights peeped through the frilly leaves of a border of geraniums and through the still blue oval of the hotel pool.

'Fern!' She gave a small frustrated cry as Connor caught up and pulled her round to face him. 'Why the devil didn't you tell me?' he demanded, his features harshly austere in the lights thrown up from the pool.

'Why the hell should I?' Anger sparkled in her eyes, loose blonde tendrils curling damply against her face in the humid night air. 'You'd made up your own mind what was wrong with me, without giving me a chance to explain. And anyway, I felt so ill at the time I couldn't have said much if I'd wanted to.'

She made to pull away, but he held her there, his eyes giving nothing away as they made a contemplative study of her face, then a slow, colour-raising survey of her slender figure. 'Was it brought on because of a row with your... lover?'

He wasn't letting up on her supposed liaison with Greg, and breathing a small sigh, she muttered, 'Yes,' and then, seeing the way those eyes darkened, feeling the increasing bite of his fingers on her soft flesh, she added quickly, 'but not for any reason you think.'

Surprisingly, he released her, waiting for her to continue, the silence filled by the roll of the ocean, the slamming of car doors, by the soft chatter and laughter drifting down to them from the terrace. And quietly, now that he was giving her the chance, she explained, 'Greg and I were friends, that was all. Business colleagues and friends. I thought he was great—I trusted him,' she said with emphasis, the hurt she had known from his disloyalty and deception showing now in pained lines across her face. Briefly then she went on to tell Connor how she had come to be in his flat in the first place, how she had only found out a few hours previously that Greg was married and what his real intentions were. 'I think he only told me the truth then because he knew I'd be working for his father-in-law,' she surmised aloud, disgust trickling through her words, 'probably thinking I was smitten enough to fall for his proposition, only I wasn't.' And with a withering glance at Connor, 'It's against my principles.'

Perhaps the discovery of how wrongly he had judged her piqued, because none too gently he caught her arm, hustling her between the buildings on to a shrub-hemmed path at the rear, until the voices on the terrace were a distant burr against the whistling frogs and crickets, and the sudden hum of a plane passing overhead, a twinkling of coloured lights disappearing into the star-studded night.

'Why didn't you tell me all this in the first place?' He didn't sound or look too pleased with her, Fern thought with a little shudder, deciding that it was his own inaccurate judgement that was needling him—the way he'd been made to look a fool—because she had done nothing wrong. 'All right, so you weren't in a fit state to communicate with me when I came in that night,' he accepted, staring down at her as though she were a brainless child. 'But you could have set the record straight the following morning—or at some stage when you realised that we were to be working together, coming here.'

'Why?' Fern looked at him obliquely, her neck and shoulders bathed golden from the lantern-spangled walls. 'To spare you from appearing like a prize idiot?' He didn't answer, but his lips thinned—whether in anger with her or with himself, she wasn't sure. But knowing she'd be unwise to rub it in, she hastened to elucidate. 'The fact of it was, I didn't think it was really any of your business. You were acting like such a first-rate pig that morning in your flat, jumping to all the wrong conclusions, that I decided to let you go on believing them since it gave you such obvious pleasure to do it. When I did find out who you were that day Franklin took me to lunch—tried to explain—you wouldn't listen. You thought I was saying it just to save my job at the agency.'

He wasn't beyond self-derision, she noted from the way that emotion manifested itself in the briefest tug of his lips. His voice, however, was calm, with no loss of self-possession as, slipping a hand into his trouser pocket, he answered, 'A natural assumption, don't you think?'

He was right, of course. But, unwilling to admit as much, she advised with far less composure than he seemed to possess, 'Just never *assume* anything, Connor,' her flint-edged response causing that firm mouth to curve slightly in the oddest of smiles, while his gaze held hers with infuriating superiority for a man who had just been shown up for what he was.

'And you never do, I suppose?'

It was a cool counterstroke, one that had her considering its relevance before she shrugged, saying, 'Sometimes. But I never act on assumptions in the pigheaded way you did. Make all the wrong deductions without hearing the other person's side first.'

A thick eyebrow arched. 'No?'

'No!' she stated adamantly. Her parents had taught her never to make judgements about people without knowing all the facts first, and she liked to think she had always acted at least on that piece of respected parental advice.

Connor's mouth twitched, and he looked about to say something more on the subject. But then he sighed, 'Why the hell are we arguing? Our mutual...misunderstanding has already cost us a lot more wasted energy than was necessary, as well as nearly losing me the best art director I could ever hope to have had.'

A warm glow began to steal through Fern from that last complimentary remark, but more from that deepening sexual awareness as his eyes caught and held hers. Swallowing to ease the dryness in her throat, she strove to find something to say, but no words would come, and she saw him smile—aware of the pulsing conflict inside her.

He lifted a hand to her cheek, his fingers moving with a heart-stopping lightness down the delicate curve of her jaw.

'You know, you were a fool holding back, Fern,' through a haze of dizzying emotion she heard his warm, husky voice convey. 'And perhaps an even bigger one confessing it now.'

Her heart lurched and doubled its pace as he lifted both hands to the clasp at the nape of her neck, and then, like the Prince of Darkness stripping his willing victim of her last shred of immunity, removed the heavy piece of jewellery with mocking ease. She felt naked, exposed—and, in the clutches of a blazing primeval excitement, she understood what he meant. She had surrendered her only shield against him when she had told him about Greg, she thought hazily, watching him pocket the treasure as if it were worthless—and he must surely know she felt nothing for Ross. There were no barriers between them now.

His mouth coming down on hers was affirmation of that fact, his arms crushing her against his lean, hard length in an unmistakable statement of possession.

She wanted to resist. To show him that she objected strongly to the way he had treated her and that he couldn't just kiss her and pretend everything was all right. But she had no means of defence, and all too eagerly her body responded to its welcome victor, straining towards him, her mind too ready, as his lips left hers to play along the soft, warm column of her neck, to acknowledge that no other man had ever made her feel— could ever make her feel—like this.

'Shall we go down to the beach?' His voice was ragged with need, making her pulses race, her own desire a burning poignancy in her loins that she strove to bring under control. He was only suggesting a walk, after all! Nevertheless, her heart continued to pound as he casually took her hand to lead her downhill, past the fairy-lit cottages, to the sea.

She could smell it even from here—tangy and fresh; still hear it, too, even though it was hidden from view by the hotel buildings, its thunderous roar tempered by the soft sibilance of the waves scurrying back over the sand. But it was the reptiles that claimed ascendancy inland, their piercing chorus emanating from every tree and shrub along the path, and Fern tugged away from those warm fingers clasping hers, drawn by a whistling so close at hand that it had her eagerly scanning a spiky-leafed palm to find the source.

'Looking for the frog?' He laughed at her childlike enthusiasm to find the little songster as he came with that slow, easy grace to her side.

'I've got to see *one*!' she breathed in laughing response, unable to add that she needed these moments to still the pounding in her blood—then glanced up as a door closed a little way down the path and someone came out of one of the cottages.

'You'll be lucky.' The man, an American, grinned at them, aware, as he strode past. 'This is my fifth vacation here and I've never yet been able to spot one of those little fellas!'

'Because he doesn't know how,' Connor supplied in smiling conspiracy when the man had gone by. 'It's easy when you do. Just locate the sound...' He bent down to where the shrill whistle was coming from, that handsome face dark with concentration, making Fern's heart skip as it angled close to hers. 'Now look for the glistening. You should be able to see it quite clearly in this subdued light.'

And suddenly there it was. A perfect, miniature frog, its dark, shiny body no more than an inch long, clinging to its leaf with tiny, suckered feet.

'Oh, it's superb!' Excited, Fern kept her voice to a whisper, half afraid the little creature might take fright and disappear, watching, surprised, as a small sac suddenly inflated under its chin, and its body puffed out to emit its familiar shrill whistle, taking on the appearance of two appealingly tiny balloons. 'So that's how they do it!' she breathed, enthralled. 'Now I can tell everyone I've actually seen one!'

'It makes you that happy?' Her delight in something so simple seemed to surprise him, his indulgent smile stirring such an ache of yearning in her veins that she started to move away, back to the path. 'Stay here.' It hung as a soft command on the night-scented air. 'I want to remember you here—looking like this.'

His eyes probed the tense youthfulness of her face, caressing the wild tumble of her hair, impaling her, though his words had had a ring of impermanency to them that made her feel strangely low. Surely she wasn't imagining anything lasting between them, was she? she wondered chasteningly. He might have accepted the truth about her now, but she'd be laying herself open to certain heartache if she started imagining she could be anything special to him after what Ross had told her today.

'You're beautiful.' Her common sense fled as he reached for her, his hands gently caressing her shoulders. 'No wonder Greg was driven to risk his marriage for the chance to take you to bed!'

The reminder made her stiffen, her hands against the dark sleeves of his jacket, trying to hold him away. Did he still think she had encouraged Greg in some way? Put him in a position where he hadn't been able to stop himself propositioning her?

'Oh, it isn't your fault,' he advised sagely, reading her mind, the dim lights revealing the flush of restrained passion in his cheeks. 'You've got something that's beyond being simply attractive to a man, and I'm not going to explain what it is. And I don't see why that should make you blush,' he noted quietly as she succeeded in freeing herself and he came after her down the path. 'I would have thought you were far too sophisticated for that.' And suddenly, unexpectedly, 'How many men have you known, Fern? Or is it being too imprudent to ask?'

Her small, trapped breath was drowned by the boilers breaking over the reef beyond the beach. What could she tell him? I'm still a virgin? He probably wouldn't believe her. Or worse, drop her like a hot potato when he realised she didn't possess anywhere near the degree of his own expertise.

Instead, ignoring his question, she enquired shakily, 'What *is* that?' because the path had brought them between the last of the cottages and in front of them stood a vertical stone circle—a gateway framing the steps leading down to the floodlit beach and the surf-crested reefs beyond. 'I've seen several of these in gardens across the island. Do they have any particular significance?' she asked, glad of the diversion.

'It's called a moongate,' he told her, smiling. 'When a couple walk through it, legend demands they should make a wish.' The hand that clasped hers sent a fresh wave of excitement coursing through her. 'Shall we?' he invited with a glance towards the lovers' gate.

It was a whimsical exercise, but its import lay heavily with her as she crossed the threshold with him. Would he have done the same thing with Madree? With Sabrina? Oh, heaven, she hoped not! And wondered why it mattered as she tripped lightly down the rugged steps beside him, then stooped to remove her shoes, feeling the soft, cool sand between her toes.

'Well, did you make a wish?' asked Connor.

Had she? she reflected, and, realising, made light of it with a laughing, 'Now that would be telling! Did you?' Breathless words, because he had dipped his head, making her heart jerk in her breast as he gathered her against him, the lips that claimed hers incredibly arousing, unbelievably tender.

'It's already been granted,' he whispered, and kissed her again, this time with more urgency, locking them in a time-warp with the moon and the sand and the ageless ocean, two figures silhouetted against the rocks.

Deeply in love, Fern thought, to anyone watching on the terrace where they themselves had stood minutes before. No one would know that until tonight Connor had despised her totally, nor would they care, any more than she did in her abandoned acceptance of his warm hands sliding down her body, moulding her to him, her senses seduced by the fragrant night and those lips that had suddenly found the cool, bare curve of her shoulder, evoking a need in her as primitive and dangerous as the reef.

'Connor...' Beneath the soft fabric of his suit she felt his hardening response, and she arched against him in that age-old gesture of submission of the female for her chosen mate. She knew he had other women—that his inability to commit himself to one sprang from his understandable mistrust of her sex. And yet knowing that she still wanted him, so much that the emotional and physical upheaval of her senses was too much in her fragile state. That familiar ache throbbed across her temple, enough to bring her to her senses, and she murmured in a voice trembling with emotion, 'What about Madree?'

Reluctantly, it seemed, Connor held her away from him so that he could look at her, the absence of his body warmth a gaping chasm inside her. 'I told you—she's just a friend.'

Something stabbed at her heart as well as her head as she retorted, 'A very special one who makes you rush off to meet her the minute you get off the plane!'

The thick brows knitted in a frown, changing to a slow, dawning smile. 'My love, what a vivid imagination you have! I was coming here to see Williams to finalise co-ownership of this hotel—and you thought...' His unfinished sentence ran into a deep sigh. 'I'm really not the only one who jumps to conclusions, am I? Still, I should have guessed when you virtually accused me of hopping into bed with her that first morning on the *Host*.'

'Don't tell me it wasn't a temptation. She said herself you promised to go back down——'

'To sort out the coffee-maker,' amazingly she heard him justifying. 'It wasn't working properly and I said I'd try to fix it.' Gently he drew her back to him, back into the exquisite haven of his arms. 'Would I have decided to join you in the water that day if I'd been planning a stolen hour of sin with her?' There was a soft admonishment in his words, tender against her hair. 'What do you think I am, my sweet, some sort of sexual gymnast?'

A small murmur of joy, of ecstasy, bubbled from her lips. So Madree was no longer a rival! And Sabrina?

She couldn't say it—bring herself to ask him. Besides, she told herself, England was a long, long way away. Apart from which, she didn't want to destroy the magic his questing lips and hands were suddenly creating for her, except that something else was dampening the wild ecstasy in her blood—pulsing cruelly across her temple so that she dropped her head against the cushioning warmth of Connor's shoulder with a small, involuntary groan of pain.

'What is it, Fern?' She didn't want to tell him, not wanting to make a fuss. But then he said swiftly, 'Of course. As if I don't know.' And with a hard lifting of his chest, 'I'm taking you back to the hotel.'

He'd misunderstood, she thought, feeling that restlessness in him as he held her against him all the way back in the taxi, her heart thumping like her head as he brought her to her door.

With a pained, nervous excitement, she watched him unlock it. Would he, because she'd shown herself to be so receptive to his kisses, automatically assume that she would...?

'Goodnight, Fern.'

As the door swung open, she sent an upward glance at him, surprise in her tired features. And he said quietly, 'I'm not Greg. Or Ross,' he added as an afterthought. 'I won't seduce a woman just because the opportunity presents itself. You aren't in any fit state for love-making—not tonight, anyway.'

And that was that? Fern thought dazedly, as he took her hand, pressing her key into her palm and, closing her fingers around it, lifted the small clenched fist to his lips, their warmth lingering for breath-catching seconds on her skin before he turned and strode away.

CHAPTER EIGHT

THE succeeding week was a combination of hard work and euphoria, as Fern saw all her team's compilation of ideas for ALI's new products taking shape, romanticised by the sheer magic of design, technique and camera—with the further and greater thrill of all her spare time being claimed by its chief executive.

He took her sailing on the *Host*, engaging the services of a surprisingly discreet crew. But though she and Connor were left to themselves most of the time, he didn't make love to her on his yacht, calling a halt to their kisses and light petting—that only he seemed to be in control of—as soon as it threatened to get out of hand. It was as though he was taking their relationship a step at a time, giving them a chance to get to know each other properly, to develop friendship before anything more serious after all the misunderstanding and mutual antagonism that had gone before.

At his side she saw crew members, hoteliers and waiters alike bend, as her own team had, to that authority that came only from being immensely rich and powerful. And yet, in spite of it, she could be herself with him, she discovered, forgetting how successful he was—who he was—in the overwhelming pleasure of his company. He could be great fun too, surprising her one day when he suggested hiring some transport and doing an overland tour of the island, and waiting, as arranged, in the sunshine outside the hotel, Fern burst into astonished laughter as he drew up alongside her on a moped.

'Oh, no! Whatever do you look like?' She doubled up with laughter, paralysed by continual fresh bursts every time she tried to straighten up, but she couldn't help it. Connor McManus on a moped was something she hadn't envisioned at all.

'I'll tell you something even funnier.' With lips compressing in wry amusement, he tossed her a spare helmet. 'You're getting on the back.'

'Oh, spare me, *please*!' She was still laughing at him, though now it was more just a show of enjoying herself at his expense, because in truth he looked sensational. Helmeted, with a short-sleeved denim shirt and tight white Bermuda shorts hugging those powerful legs, he reminded her of a ruthlessly handsome American speed-cop—the type who would flay the skin off your bones for doing thirty in a twenty-five-mile restriction.

'I'll spare you in a minute.' Against the twittering of sparrows on the hotel terrace above the portico, Connor's deep voice held a delicious promise. 'It's a long way to St George's, and if you don't want a sore seat before we get there I suggest you get on now.'

'Aye, aye, sir!' She saluted him in mock obedience and, helmeted herself now, felt his gaze, hot as the sun's rays, brush appreciatively over her legs in her flattering blue shorts as she sat astride the bike.

'Now hold on tight.'

Willingly, she thought, knowing a small thrill just from putting her arms around his firm, warm waist, and then it felt as if they were taking off, the buzz of the bike's engine joining with the purring contentment in her heart as they turned out of the hotel grounds and Connor opened up with full throttle along the leafy, oleander-lined lanes.

The smell of Bermuda, Fern thought, her hair blowing out from beneath her helmet as she turned to admire the pink blossoms, inhaling the powdery sweetness of the warm morning air.

It was only just over twenty miles to the island's old capital, and yet, surprisingly, Connor told her it would probably take a good hour—mainly, she discovered, because often one couldn't maintain the twenty-two-mile speed-limit through the tiny, picturesque villages, but also because they kept stopping at convenient points to drink in the sheer beauty of the island; the delicate and varying colours of the houses with their familiar white roofs; the unexpected view of a bay; a poinciana tree in someone's front garden, its dense cluster of scarlet flowers a flaming crown beneath the dazzling blue of the sky; pausing, too, to sniff the wild blooms that grew in profusion in every thicket and hedge beside the road.

'Oh, look! What are these?' They were riding along what had used to be one of the island's many old railway tracks and which had been utilised as a narrow lane for joggers, walkers and motorcyclists since trains, Connor had explained earlier, hadn't survived as a viable source of transport in Bermuda. Now he drew up beneath the tree Fern had indicated, and she followed his example, getting off the bike to stretch her legs. 'Aren't they beautiful?' she whispered, gazing up into the gently stirring branches at the bell-shaped yellow flowers, too high to reach. 'I wonder what they are.'

'Golden trumpets.' He looked smug, his eyes twinkling mischievously so that she didn't know if he was making it up or not. But then the breeze loosened one of the fragile blooms and it floated gently down, and Fern laughed at its superb timing as Connor caught it in his palm.

'Madam, whatever you desire,' he said solemnly, and, with a gallant bow, 'A flower for my lady.' He placed its thin stem beneath the strap of her sun-top just below her shoulder, gold against the flimsy white cotton. Her pulse quickened from the casual brush of his fingers on her bare arm, racing as he suddenly stooped to kiss her, but with such a clash of helmets that they both burst out laughing, his laughter complementing the high, silvery note of hers, deep and resonant along the deserted hibiscus-hedged trail.

After that the day seemed to take on a new kind of perfection, Fern decided, laughing aloud at the crabs that scuttled out of the grassy verges along the South Shore, vividly pink bodies taking refuge in the dense undergrowth that sloped down to the coral-pink beaches and the placid sea.

They arrived in the ancient capital to find an old-world atmosphere—many of the locals were dressed in seventeenth-century English costume and tourists were posing for photographs in the ancient cedar stocks that stood on the colourful colonial square.

'Do you want me to take your photograph with your head and hands incarcerated?' The deep voice was laced with mirth over the clamouring peal of a magnificent town-crier's bell.

Laughing, Fern shook her head, instantly dismissing the idea. 'Why do I get the impression that then I'd be exactly where you want me?' she murmured, but on a slightly breathless note as she headed for a gift shop window on the other side.

'Now there you're quite wrong, sweetheart.' Her pulse leaped as Connor's arm slid around her shoulders, drawing her against the granite-hewn strength of his side. 'I'm planning a far more sophisticated form of torture for you.'

Brown eyes met hazel, flickering with laughter and such an obvious sensual promise that she felt herself blushing and wondered if he could feel the way her heart was beating, like a metronome out of control.

They had lunch—the biggest pizza Fern had ever seen in her life—outdoors under the canopy of a stone-built restaurant overlooking the harbour where small sailing boats and other craft idled in the sheltering arm of Bermuda's famous town. A shower started, light, welcome raindrops blowing under the canopy, as cool and refreshing as the golden lagers they had ordered, packed with ice. Then it was over, and the hot, bright sunshine regained superiority as they resumed their exploration of the town.

A look over the replica of the earliest settlers' ship inspired Fern to know more of the Colony's history, and, on the way back to the dockside where they had left the moped, Connor told her, painting an interesting picture for her with his expert knowledge of the convening of Bermuda's first government in 1620, the island's part in past trade and how the very parish where their hotel was situated was named after the Englishman who had led those sea survivors to safety eleven years before.

'Theirs wasn't the first ship—or the last,' he appended with a grimace, 'to be ripped apart by the reefs. There have been countless casualties since—frigates, steamships, fishing sloops—even private chartered yachts during recent years.'

Fern pulled a wry face as she watched him unlocking the scooter. 'You're beginning to sound like Ross!' she teased. 'He's a maritime dictionary!'

Watching her, those eyes were like dark liquid honey in the sunlight. 'Do I detect a note of exasperation, Fern?' With a smooth efficiency he had resumed that breath-catching speed-cop image. 'Are you calling poor Ross a reef-wreck bore?'

'There's nothing poor about Ross!' she laughed, repositioning her own helmet. 'He's easily as rich as you are!' Millionaires together, she thought drily, only

Connor didn't flaunt it—surround himself with tawdry embellishments in the way Ross seemed to need to.

'I see.' There was an odd twist to his lips as he stood looking down into the lively and, right then, impish youthfulness of her face. 'Is that the attraction?' he asked in a way that was both amused and castigating, and, lifting a hand to her jaw, he suddenly yanked the strap of her helmet none too gently into place.

Fern winced, her eyes suddenly dark and questioning beneath his, wounded by his intentional brutality. Of course. He would have had his share of women who couldn't resist the blend of that power-packed animal vitality with all that wealth, she thought, afraid to admit, even to herself, why he had such a profound effect on her—but it certainly wasn't because of his money.

'So you've found out!' she accused on a gasp of mock-guilt, hiding her complex emotions behind her feigned joviality, determined not to succumb to his bullying tactics, although she couldn't help wondering, with wounded speculation, whether he saw her as just another woman he couldn't trust, because of that earlier bitter relationship he'd had in the past.

Her thoughts kept her silent, more subdued than she had been on the outward journey—especially when Connor's mood seemed darker too. Consequently she was surprised when, without a word, he pulled off the road into a layby on the banks of an enchanting little inlet.

Leaning palms threw shadows on the grass from the late afternoon sun; across the small stretch of blue water marshmallow-coloured cottages gazed back on sleepily bobbing boats, their simplicity and charm somehow surprisingly complemented by the tasteful, imposing architecture of lavish modern apartments a little further down-channel.

'You like fish,' Connor remembered, bringing one long, tanned leg over the bike. 'In which case this place should be right up your street.'

She hadn't noticed before, but on the opposite side of the road stood the island's aquarium, and she felt a soaring in her blood from the way Connor caught her hand, pulling her with him across the pedestrian crossing.

His mood had changed again, she was happy to see, back to that easy light-heartedness of the morning, so that her spirits lifted too, as they viewed the silent residents of an underwater world behind the thick, wide panels of glass. Grouper, eels, even a shark, as well as one particular barracuda—decidedly fiercer-looking than its more feared companion, despite its smaller size, Fern decided—which kept turning, teeth bared, to stare disconcertingly out at her from every angle of its enormous tank so that she backed away, wheeling round with a small gasp straight into Connor's arms.

'It won't stop looking at me!' she breathed with a laughing shudder, and met an answering amusement in those brown eyes—and something else that made her heart flip wildly.

'Can you blame it?'

'You . . . !' She pushed at him playfully, her laughter tremulous then, because one strong arm had wrapped itself protectively around her and she could feel the heat of him beneath her palms, emanating from under the soft denim shirt.

Desire licked along her veins, an aching sweetness through her body that would only be soothed by the unleashing of the raw, primitive needs she could feel in him—read so clearly in the dark, febrile glitter of his eyes. He smiled, and she sucked in a breath as his lips brushed her temple, her senses clinging to the scent and feel and warmth of him, her mind wishing fervently that the rest of the visitors to the aquarium would spirit themselves away so that she could feel those hard arms tighten uncompromisingly around her, feel those strong lean hands caressing, moulding...

'Had enough?'

His voice broke the spell, and she was glad to don her sunglasses to hide the havoc of emotion inside her as she let Connor lead her out into the small zoological garden in the almost painful brightness of the afternoon.

'Oh, look at those giant tortoises! I used to have one of those.' She was gazing eagerly into the small area housing several majestic specimens, experiencing a sharp pang of sympathy for them stranded so far from their natural home.

'What did you do? Have the garden extended by a mile or two?' Behind her those deep tones teased, the lines of laughter in his face giving it a warmth she wanted to drown in.

'You knew what I meant!' she chided good humouredly, thinking back to the collection of pets she had acquired as a child—budgerigars, rabbits and guinea-pigs, besides the tiny lovable tortoise that had outlived them all. 'It had the whole run of the garden, as Dad didn't grow anything that couldn't be mowed or pruned, and by some coincidence a very friendly tortoiseshell cat used to come into our garden—and on one occasion when I was out there sunbathing she snuggled down beside me and what I presume she must have thought was a very smooth rounded stone. You should have seen her face,' Fern remembered, her own breaking into smiles, 'when halfway through the afternoon the "stone" suddenly got up and walked away!'

'I can imagine.' With a lop-sided grin, Connor slid an arm around her shoulders, the gesture casual and easy, yet it started Fern's heart pumping at twice its normal pace. Her blood raced from the thrill of his glorious closeness, the musky-tinged warmth of his body, as he guided her unhurriedly around the little zoo. After a while, though, leaning comfortably against the lean, hard angle of his side began to feel natural, so she relaxed, laughing with him at the antics of a small seal as it splashed playfully into the depths of a murky pool beside which its larger companions dozed, regardless, skins shining like satin in the sun.

Unconsciously she edged closer to him near the large reptile pen, where copiously toothed alligators with gnarled, leathery bodies basked, still as statues, beneath the glittering blue sky.

'Would it surprise you to learn that I spent some time in a zoo?'

Fern looked up at him, mischief quickly replacing surprise. 'As keeper or inmate?' she jested, shrieking as she was thrust towards the wall that separated them from those dark, deadly bodies, only to be pulled back against Connor's, his arms encircling her, his voice thrilling and deep in her ear.

'I feed rude little girls like you to the lions,' he breathed in mock remonstration. Then more seriously, 'I took a job for a few months mucking out cages between university and going abroad, though heaven knows why! I've always found these places more repellent than entertaining,' he went on above a sudden, ear-splitting cacophony from an aviary on the other side of the gardens. 'With television providing every nature programme imaginable and the increasing number of nature reserves springing up everywhere these days, it strikes me as a rather outdated practice that we still find it necessary to inflict treatment on other innocent species that we'd flinch from inflicting on the most hardened of our own kind.'

From the curve of his arm Fern gazed up at him, her eyes softening with an emotion that was as warming as the sun on her face and arms. He was right, she thought, murmuring her agreement, totally in accord with what he had said. He was tougher than most men she had met, calculatingly ruthless when put to the test—because hadn't she had a taste of his obdurate and unrelenting contempt herself? But beneath that outer shell of hard, self-sufficient masculinity there was vulnerability, too—concern and caring, the things he had just said proving it, stirring feelings in her that went beyond basic respect and fondness and which, with that glaring physical attraction, compounded to make him the most desirable, exciting and wonderful man she had ever known in her life. And suddenly, there among the grinning alligators and sleepy seals, she realised that she loved him, that she would always love him—and that, crazy though it seemed, the most important thing to her now was for Connor McManus to be in love with her.

The warm spray of the shower was a refreshing tingle over her body as she stood, reliving the precious hours she had spent in Connor's company. The ride to St George's. That romantic gesture when he'd given her that flower—his sense of humour. And that devastating moment in the zoo when she had woken up to just how deep her feelings for him were.

Her acknowledgement of those emotions had left her oddly dazed, shaken, so that she had been decidedly taciturn with him on the journey back. Perhaps, though, Connor couldn't have had any idea of the reason for her unusual reticence, she thought, and for now, at least, she wanted to keep it that way. Oh, she couldn't deny that for the first time in her life she was ready for a serious relationship with a man. That she wanted to go to bed with him. Make love with him! she accepted shamelessly, feeling a tingling of a more intrinsic kind as the water cascaded down over her suddenly aching breasts. But a sexual relationship wasn't a thing she could enter into lightly, she ruminated, ignoring the throb deep in her loins as mental pictures rose before her mind's eye of the glorious act of submission to him, his flesh pressing against hers, the sweet hard thrust of possession...

No, there were things to think about—like her career, and unwanted pregnancy. It was all she could do to try and dampen the stimulating effects of her imagery by submerging herself totally under the shower. She didn't intend jeopardising her career, ruining her life, for a few sublime moments of ecstasy with a man. She would be wisely prepared before she would even consider anything like that. And anyway, Ross might have said that Connor didn't trust women any more, but Franklin had called Sabrina 'the lady in his life', and even if Connor had denied any commitment to her, as well as Madree, doubt still niggled at the back of Fern's mind.

She brushed the water out of her eyes, hearing the call of some exotic bird in the grounds outside. Yes, there it was, she noticed, peering above the shower curtain through the open, meshed window—a cardinal perched high in one of the date palms overlooking the pool. Blood red. Red for danger, she thought dramatically with a grimace, directing the warning wryly at herself—then literally shrieked as the plastic curtain was suddenly ripped back, exposing her to the hard gaze of the man whose eyes were burning across her body like hot, angry coals.

CHAPTER NINE

'EXACTLY!' Connor erupted, his swift, hard assessment of her defensive pose—arms crossed over her breasts, one knee drawn up towards her body—lifting to her large frightened eyes, her face, drained of all colour, beneath her dripping hair. 'I could have been any man,' he rasped, his anger roused and censuring. 'Do you make it your normal practice to take a shower with your door not only unlocked but with your key left on the outside?'

Which was thoroughly careless, Fern realised when her brain began to function normally again, wondering how she could have been so negligent as she grabbed the curtain he'd now released, using it as a shield against her nakedness. 'You could have knocked!' she exclaimed.

'Believe me, I did! And hard,' he stated in harsh reprimand, obviously aware of the embarrassed colour she could feel creeping back into her cheeks before his gaze fell, lingering unsettlingly on the expanse of creamy-gold flesh she was trying, rather ineffectually, to conceal.

'I didn't hear you,' she uttered unnecessarily, calmer now.

'Obviously not.' With that dry remark, his gaze was tugging down over the revealing transparent plastic so that Fern swallowed, suddenly aware of her body's betrayal of her, of her breasts, still heavy from desirous thoughts of the man her imagination had somehow conjured up. 'I thought you might be missing this.' It was her purse, which she hadn't realised she'd mislaid, and which had probably got mixed up with his things in the basket on the back of the bike, she assumed, as Connor tossed it down on the vanity shelf under the wide mirror.

'Thanks,' she said sheepishly, guessing from that askance look he gave her that he was wondering why she had suddenly become so absentminded. And the last thing she was going to do was tell him! 'I'll lock your door from the outside and slip the key back underneath,' he stated, and with a lazy, appreciative survey of her, remarked, 'That is…unless of course you'd prefer me…to stay.'

Fern couldn't answer. Nor did he expect her to, she realised, her whole body aching, pulsing with a feverish anguish as he gave her a lop-sided smile and turned away.

'Connor.' Above the cascade of the shower, she hardly recognised her own voice, something beyond her will seeming to reach out, spurring her on from her desperate, reckless longing to detain him.

His eyes seemed to consume her as she turned round, and a black eyebrow arched in silent, partially surprised enquiry.

Fern's tongue strayed across her top lip. He was waiting, but no words would come. She was too inexperienced for this game, she thought hopelessly, her mouth going dry, the pounding of her blood making her dizzy, making her wish she hadn't taken this unwise, abandoned path, that he would take the lead, before he murmured in tones thick and husky with desire, 'Want me to wash your back?'

Oh, *did* she! Only the hunger in her eyes drew him to her, her sensibilities engulfed by the flame of excitement that was licking along her veins, the wild anticipation now that he had taken control.

'What are you doing?' On a trembling, astonished whisper she watched him kick off his shoes and step, fully clothed, into the shower with her, dark patches already forming on his shirt from the relentless spray.

'There's a sign over there...' he jerked a glance towards the basin '...that says "Water's precious—don't waste it". So I think we ought to start economising, don't you?'

The amused tug of his lips was at variance with the dark, brooding emotion in his eyes, and if, sensing her tension, he had defused the situation somewhat by the craziness of his action, he ignited rockets inside her as he pulled her into his arms.

Every part of her being seemed to explode in a paroxysm of need, and she surrendered to that hard mouth over hers with a small, strangled cry of desire.

The water was saturating them, drowning the sound of their quickened breathing, and Fern sighed into his mouth, feeling her breasts swelling, their hardening tips sensitised by the soaking coarse denim of Connor's shirt. It was a stimulus in itself, being naked while he still had the advantage of his clothes. Like slave and master, she thought through the frightening grip of her desire, the warmth of his hands over the slippery-soaped satin of her body arousing her to such a pitch that she writhed against him with total abandonment, driven by the needles of wanting that were arrowing through her breasts, and the sweet, moist ache between her thighs.

'God, what you do to me!' Against the tumbling water, Connor's voice was an anguished groan. Gently his lips moved down the sensitive column of her throat, and Fern felt her legs buckle under her, only Connor's strength holding her up as he bent his mouth to take the throbbing pinnacle of her breast into his mouth.

What *she* did to *him*! Her fingers curled tensely into the taut muscles of his shoulders, clutching at his solid warmth as his arm tightened around her bare midriff, angling her against him so that he could taste the wet softness of her body with greater ease.

'You look so young. So beautiful and so...innocent...'
His voice sounded hoarse, his eyes slumbrous beneath
the heavy sable of his lashes as he teased a tendril of her
dripping hair, twisting it around her finger before gently
caressing the softness of her wet cheek with the back of
his hand. 'Undress me.'

His soft command washed over her with the steady
stream of water, soft but inexorable, bringing her an-
aesthetised faculties pulsing back to life.

Tentatively she unfastened the buttons of his sodden
shirt, strangely shy of doing the thing she most wanted
to do. But desire alone ruled, and she slipped her hands
beneath the confining fabric, her fingers, tingling from
the contact with his damp, sun-soaked flesh, peeling the
shirt away from his powerful torso like a superfluous
skin.

He was beautiful, she thought, seeing the water
running in rivulets down through that dark tangle of hair
spanning his chest, the sleek velvet of his skin concealing the invincible power of steel.

'Hell, Fern!' he whispered in a voice ragged with
passion as she pressed kisses against the wet salty warmth
of his throat, his chest, a firm male nipple. 'You don't
know what you're doing to me!' But then with more
control, an indulgent curve to his mouth, he said gently,
'And the rest.'

She swallowed, her gaze dropping to the firm-muscled
leanness of his waist, to his hips in the hugging white
cotton of his Bermudas, and she hesitated, suddenly ab-
surdly shy. And then he laughed, taking over again, di-
vesting himself of his remaining garments to pull her
back against him.

'Are those innocent looks just a front, or am I going
to have to teach you?' he smiled, through a warm, enquiring surprise.

'Wouldn't you like to know?' she purred, cat-sweet and provocative—but tremblingly too, because, in truth, it was a new experience for her being naked with a man, and the sensuous warmth of his skin was producing sensations in her that had her moving urgently against him, her soft form begging for the kisses he was suddenly raining over every sensitive inch of her, inviting him, unwittingly guiding him along the undiscovered, secret pathways of her body.

Yielding to the hungry demands of his lips and hands, to the alarming potency of her own physical and emotional needs, she could only murmur her acquiescence when he said raggedly, 'Let's go into the other room.'

Swathed in towels, she was being placed gently down on the single bed, the cooler air, stirred by the ceiling fan, welcoming after the hot, steamy atmosphere of the shower. Needing more, though, than the tender teasing of his mouth on hers, she tried to draw him down to her, her young, turban-framed face flushed with wanting, frustration a soft burst from her lips as he suddenly denied her the sweet ecstasy of his kisses and sat up.

'Patience, darling.' He smiled wanly down at her, the gesture undermined by some other powerful emotion that caused that hard expansion of his chest and put that look of tense need in his face.

A towel slung low across his hips, his torso was still wet, glistening bronze beneath the hairs curling damply against his skin. He inhaled deeply, as if to gain more command over himself, and then, very purposefully, he parted the pristine white bath sheet that was wrapped around her, those thick lashes lowered as he gazed down on the naked golden vista of her body.

'You're so very lovely...' His eyes were full of dark emotion, the strong cast of his cheek and jaw softened by his silent appreciation of her—a visual caress so highly sensual that it dragged a small sound from her throat.

'Oh, please...' Aroused, demented for him, Fern reached up to touch the cool dampness of his hair, the rough, unshaven line of his cheek. 'Please love me!'

But he was making her wait—deliberately, she realised, and tentatively she smiled up at him, needing him, her love for him mirrored in her softly vulnerable features as somewhere in the recesses of her consciousness she remembered the warning she had made to herself about precautions—abandoning it in a haze of heated anticipation that vowed to end in delirium as soon as Connor touched her—which it did, bringing her sobbing and gasping, straining against his rousing masculine warmth, consumed by a furnace of tormenting need that could only be assuaged by the hard, thrusting power of his body.

The sudden full weight of him was like a time-bomb to her mindless senses, and desire guided her by instinct so that her legs parted for him spontaneously like the petals of some erotic flower for the sun.

His skin clung damply to hers, her softly perspiring flesh responding to him with breath-catching sensitivity beneath his stroking, probing hands. But all of a sudden he was easing himself up, his features taut with summoned control, looking as if he had just dragged himself back from the precipice of eternal pleasure as, in a voice raw with emotion, he breathed, 'Before we do this...I'd better know——'

The shrill ring of the telephone beside the bed interrupted whatever he had been going to say, cutting startlingly through Fern's comatosed reasoning.

In the clutches of her sensual bonds, she couldn't move even to pick it up, and after a few seconds Connor reached over, his voice remarkably steady, then surprisingly familiar with whoever was on the other end of the line.

'Franklin,' he told her, his hand clamped over the mouthpiece. And with a wry movement of lips, 'He wants to know what I'm doing in your room.'

'For heaven's sake!' she hissed, embarrassed, as he handed her the receiver, sitting up and grasping the bath sheet to her as though Franklin Stone might have visual powers beyond the norm.

'Don't trust him, sweetheart.' It was an amused, avuncular scepticism, coming surprisingly clearly across the Atlantic. 'He's got the killer instinct of a shark. Apart from which, I've got no intention of losing a second brilliant art director this side of Christmas!' She could picture his ample midriff shaking as his distinctive laughter boomed across the miles. 'What was that?'

You wouldn't believe it! Fern thought, tensing, trying to stifle a second small gasp as she felt Connor's tongue moving lightly down the sensitive length of her spine.

'Stop it!' she insisted in whispered protest, and was mortified to catch Franklin's enquiring,

'What did you say?'

'No-thing—I sneezed,' she lied jerkily, with a sudden, involuntary straightening of her back, because that warm, moist tongue had found the gentle curve of her waist, and with such arousing skill that it was all she could do not to sigh her pleasure down the phone.

'Unfortunately I'm going to have to call you back to the office immediately,' dismayed, Fern heard her employer suddenly informing her. 'I've got two people out this end with summer flu, one of the designers has had a row with one of my partners and walked out, and we've got clients screaming for their artwork by the end of the week! You've done a splendid PR job out there, Fern, but Jenny can organise the remaining photo sessions quite adequately on her own. I want you on a plane back—tonight,' he was advising with dogged insistence. 'You'll be far more use to me here than out there with Connor McManus.'

'Tonight?' Fern echoed, deflated, knowing she had no choice as she tried to wriggle out of Connor's grasp. The bed creaked as he desisted his sweet torture of her senses and sat up, dark brows knitting as he realised what the other man was demanding.

'Tell him to go back to bed or go and pester someone else,' he drawled in amiable protest across the soft-scented slope of her shoulder, reminding her, through a delicious, shuddering pleasure, that it had to be getting on for midnight in England.

'What's he saying? Put him on.' There was an almost paternal impatience in the disembodied voice, and, with a defeated little shrug at Connor, Fern complied.

'All right, all right. I'll see she's on the plane,' Connor placated Franklin after a few moments, holding the phone in the crook of his neck, while his hands continued to explore her body with a very determined life of their own. 'No, I still haven't compounded my ideas for the new yachting brochure, but I'll come and discuss them with you the day after I get back. I'll call in on my way to the college, and we can also discuss the designs for that face lift...'

Fern closed her ears to the rest, her body suddenly rigid beneath those warm, roving hands, and, purposefully now, she pulled away from them, wrapping her towel around her sarong-style as she got up from the bed.

Of course. Connor still had a life in England, and a girlfriend who was part of that life, those casual words had cruelly reminded her. Even if his relationship with the woman was as noncommittal as he'd said it was, it still existed. And how did she know that she herself wasn't just another casual relationship for him? After all, he hadn't said he cared for her in any way, and he was an extremely attractive man who knew he could always attract women—sophisticated, beautiful women like Madree. And yet a few moments ago she had been prepared to let all her principles slide . . .

The click of the phone on its rest awakened her to the fact that Connor had finished his conversation. Back stiffening, Fern gazed out through the slats of the venetian blind, staring sightlessly at the hibiscus-flecked hedges and, just visible through the trees, the white roof of the gazebo beside the pool.

Her nerves were as taut as a bow-string as Connor came up behind her, his hands sliding caressingly down the silken length of her arms.

'Now where were we?' he breathed, his lips so softly sensual on the too readily receptive column of her throat that she dragged in her breath, her senses enslaved by that familiar scent of his warm, near-naked body, the cool touch of his wet black hair against her cheek.

'Packing.' From somewhere she summoned up enough will-power to make herself say it. 'You heard him. I've got to be on that plane tonight.'

She tried to free herself, only to be twisted round in his arms, the feel of his hair-coarsened chest beneath her hands weakening her resistance.

'Surely we can spare an hour?' Against the towel-freed tumble of damp hair his words—his lips, as he bent to taste her shoulder—were so powerfully persuasive that she had to fight the urge to arch against him, to give in to the sensual domination of his will, and only won by the smallest scrap of hers.

'I don't want to get pregnant,' she said tonelessly, her eyes lifting to his.

'I thought you'd already taken that into consideration. That's why I nearly . . .' A small crease appeared between his eyebrows. 'I wasn't sure—which is why I didn't.'

Fern swallowed. 'Well, I haven't,' she admitted, wondering what he would think. That she was thoroughly irresponsible, probably. 'I'm not protected,' she added lamely.

The soft whirring of the fan over their heads filled the silence, and outside, voices drifted up in cheerful Caribbean patois from the path.

She could feel Connor's gaze tugging over her as if he were seeing her for the first time, and his hands, moving gently over her shoulders, were caressingly tender, his mouth taking on a gentle twist. 'I could easily rectify that.'

For a moment, aroused by his hands and the sweet temptation of all he was promising, she wanted to let him, wanted to abandon herself to his exquisite love-making, but she dragged herself out of his arms with a wild, 'No!' directed more at herself than him.

'Fern, what's wrong?' Softly, behind her, Connor was trying to understand, and on a note of incredulity, 'Am I your first lover? Is that it? Are you afraid of being hurt?'

'Yes. No. I mean...' She turned round to face him, her shoulders slumping defeatedly. 'Does there have to be a reason for a woman changing her mind about sleeping with you?' she snapped, more unkindly than she had intended, she realised, when she saw the bewildered look on his face—frustrated because she couldn't tell him the truth: that it was emotional hurt she was afraid of, that she knew she would have to endure eventually if she threw herself into a casual relationship with him—the injury to her heart when he said goodbye to her, and not any physical pain he might unintentionally cause her.

'Yes, there does,' he answered her, 'if a few moments before the woman wanted it so much she was prepared to risk changing the course of her whole life just to...' He had moved away from her, flopping down exasperatedly on the bed. The towel was still slung around his hips, and Fern felt her stomach flip at the lean, muscular perfection of him, wondering at the shadow that seemed to darken his face before he murmured pensively, looking intently at the phone, 'Unless...'

'Unless what?' Fern prompted, baffled, as he looked up at her again, by the cold, hard glint in his eyes.

'Unless it bothers you that Stone should think his client's relations with his art director should have become more personal than public and you're worried that news of it might get back to Greg.'

He meant it. Unbelievably, accusation was written all over his face, and, with her hand going to her throat, Fern flung back incredulously, 'Don't be ridiculous! I told you, Greg isn't—and never has been—my lover!'

'Yes. You *told* me,' Connor agreed with deliberate emphasis, scepticism in the cool tones.

'What does that mean? That you don't believe me?' she enquired scathingly, pink colour heightening across the soft gold of her cheeks. 'Ross was right—you don't trust anyone. You've tarred every woman with the same——' She broke off abruptly, seeing the deepening grooves around his narrowing eyes and jaw.

'Did Ross say that?' Fern bit her lower lip. She hadn't intended to implicate Ross, but Connor's suspicions, the sudden revival of those old accusations had hurt like crazy, and impetuosity had got the better of her. Motionless, she couldn't look away from those cold, inscrutable eyes as he got up and took a step or two towards her—she was lost for the right reply.

'So you know the sordid details of my past,' he accepted with a careless lift of his shoulder. 'I hope you found it entertaining. But if you think I'm licking my wounds from some unwise interlude in my life, you're wrong. I'm not.'

'Then why don't you believe me?' she demanded.

His smile was cynical, his appraisal of the damp, riotous hair falling over her shoulders and the full swell of her breasts, visible above the towel, making her pulse throb in inevitable response. 'Because you're too beautiful, too provocative and too thoroughly threatening to a man's sanity,' he said censoriously, getting up from the bed. 'Let alone his self-control. And perhaps... because I find myself wanting to—far, far too much.'

Those last, softly spoken words made Fern's heart leap with sudden hope. He looked desolate, standing there, she thought wonderingly, his eyes two dark pools of emotion that seemed to be swallowing her up. He didn't trust himself—or her. Or any woman where love was concerned, despite what he had said, she thought discerningly, but a few simple words from her could change all that. If only she could be sure...

Her eyes were wide and wanting, willing him to come to her, to make it easy for her—every nerve sharpening as he took a few steps towards her, but then suddenly he seemed to think better of it. He wasn't a man to force the issue when a woman had said no, she acceded painfully, though she could feel the potency of his need like some tangible force between them—sense it in his voice, in the sharp breath he inhaled—as he uttered thickly, 'I think I'd better leave.'

Disappointment was a cold hand across her heart, even while she acknowledged how much self-discipline it had taken for him to say it.

'How?' she asked then in a small, thin voice, remembering that his clothes were lying in a soggy heap on the bathroom floor. 'Like that? Or were you planning to

borrow my négligé?' she enquired, summoning a smile,
wondering which would raise the most eyebrows—the
sight of him striding through the hotel with only a towel
round his loins or of his thoroughly masculine physique
sporting cream satin and lace.

'Which would you recommend?' he said drily, reading
her thoughts, but he was picking up the phone, giving
his name and room number before asking, 'Is my laundry
ready yet?'

Naturally it was, Fern comprehended. And naturally
he was instructing for it to be sent up to *her* room—
shirts, shorts and all his unmentionables, probably—with
no loss of dignity on his part whatsoever!

'Don't you ever get tired of being so bloody in
control?'

She couldn't contain the imprecation, but there was
a catch in her voice, because as he moved past her towards the bathroom, using the towel he had been wearing
to dry his hair, every magnificent inch of him was exposed in all its virile glory, the sinewy smoothness of his
back and shoulders tapering down to tight white but-
tocks below the darker tan line of his trunks.

'Invariably.' He paused, unashamed of his splendid
nakedness, his facial muscles tugging in hard circum-
spection at the bright colour in her cheeks. 'Get dressed,
there's a good girl,' he advised in almost rebuking tones,
'otherwise I might just find it necessary to change my
mind.'

He was still angry with her, she realised, quickly doing
as he said. And later, at the airport, when he kissed her
goodbye, his lips were ruthless and punishing, his arms
crushing her to him as if to stamp the hard impression
of his body on hers before he let her go. And then alone,
filled with mixed emotions, she was flying off into the
night.

CHAPTER TEN

FERN had been back in the office for scarcely a matter of days when Franklin came in one morning looking extremely concerned.

'I have to drive up to Yorkshire. Sarah's had an accident,' he explained quickly to Fern. A widower—it was understandable, Fern thought, that he was extremely close to his daughter, and she could detect the worry in his voice, in those unusually strained eyes. 'She's fallen downstairs. She's all right herself, but it's touch and go about the baby,' he conveyed unhappily, 'so I'm driving up to the hospital right away.' And with that he went, taking with him Fern's hopes for the baby's safety and her express assurance that she could cope with all pending matters.

'You're a gem!' He'd smiled through his anxiety, and had actually kissed her before sweeping out of the door.

Pulling a face, Fern thought how different his opinion of her might have been if Connor had imparted his original suspicions to the other man. She doubted whether she would still have a job.

As it was, she had been given a great deal of responsibility, and over the next couple of days she coped well, thriving under pressure, although she was sorry that it had to have been brought about by such unfortunate circumstances. She was delighted, therefore, when Franklin rang during the second day to say that his unborn grandchild seemed determined to stay put. 'I'll be stopping in York for another night,' he went on to tell her, 'or at least until Sarah's discharged.'

Fern worked more happily after that, the only flaw in her efficiency those moments when her thoughts strayed far too willingly to Connor. He had said he would be in touch, but she hadn't heard from him since she had been back and guessed that he was probably still away, as Jenny and Tony, sporting healthy-looking tans, had returned only two days before. It was with bated breath, therefore, that she picked up her post from the top of the meter cupboard in the hall, where Queenie always left it, that evening and saw the two packages postmarked 'Bermuda'.

Hardly waiting until she was up the stairs, the first, she discovered, was a book from Ross entitled, *A Wealth of Fortune* which, according to the hand-scrawled message on the fly-leaf, surprisingly, he had just had published, and which depicted him on the back cover, lounging handsomely at home among the glittering bounties that had helped form the source of his tremendous fortune.

Dear Ross! Still flaunting it, she thought, letting herself into her flat and chiding herself for feeling a disappointment stronger than gratitude as she began opening the second package. And this time her heart seemed to take flight.

It was a T-shirt—with no accompanying message. Just the logo emblazoned boldly across the front—'I SURVIVED A MOPED RIDE IN BERMUDA!'

There was no mistaking who had sent it. Connor!

The simplicity of his gift made her weep, and she pressed the soft garment to her lips. He was remembering, it told her, thinking of that last day they had shared together, and silently she prayed that it could possibly mean something else as well. After all, she couldn't forget what he had said that day about wanting to trust her. Had he been trying to tell her then, in some roundabout way, that he was in love with her?

The notion didn't help to quell the feverish excitement in her blood, or to help her sleep, so that she was still thinking about it in the office the following day, having accepted why he was so cagey—why he'd have doubts and suspicions. He had obviously been hurt badly before and he wasn't prepared to put his trust into a relationship very easily again, she understood, with a sharp twinge of jealousy towards the woman who had been able to affect him so deeply. But in time, she determined, as long as he gave her the chance, she would prove to him that not all women were the same...

'Hey, stop daydreaming, Fern! You've got a visitor.' Jenny's words intruded, dragging her galloping thoughts back from the golden glow of a future with Connor to elicit a small note of shock from her as Jenny showed the man into Franklin's office where Fern was standing sorting out some papers on his desk.

'Hello, Fern.'

She swallowed, glancing at the unwelcome, fair-haired figure of Greg Peters with something not far short of disdain.

'What do you want?' she demanded, picking up a file. 'I thought I made it plain——'

'I have to talk to you in private—it's important.' He sent a glance over his shoulder to ensure that Jenny had closed the door. 'You know about Sarah's accident...?' He gestured towards Franklin's vacant chair, apparently wise to where his father-in-law was, and Fern couldn't conceal her contempt.

'Yes, but I'm surprised you do,' she remarked, coming round the desk to the filing tray. 'From what I hear you're never there!'

'Now that's not fair!' She could feel him watching her as she picked up several letters that needed answering, feel him silently studying her figure beneath the stylish cream business suit and white blouse. 'Oh, I'll agree that a lot of the trouble with our marriage has been my fault, but Sarah hasn't exactly made me feel that needed,' he complained, as though that excused it all. He dropped down on to the chair opposite the more imposing lines of his father-in-law's. 'Everything she's ever wanted, Daddy's always been there to provide for her—from a job to a three-piece suite! He doesn't interfere, but I always get the feeling that Daddy's in control, and a man likes to feel some responsibility for his wife and his own possessions. That's why I started seeing other women—because I felt threatened.'

'Threatened?' Slipping the letters into the file, Fern felt her cheeks start to flame. 'And how do you think *she* feels?' she rebuked. 'Pregnant, and having to suffer an unfaithful husband! Or doesn't she know?' she quizzed, with a withering glance in his direction.

'Well, no, not yet...that is...she's got her suspicions,' Greg faltered, without meeting Fern's gaze. 'Some female friend of hers saw me with you one lunchtime——'

'Oh, for heaven's sake!' How on earth had she got herself into this situation—and so innocently too? Damn Greg! she thought vehemently, wincing as he went on,

'They told her I was carrying on with some kid of a blonde down here in London—and that's what we were arguing about when she went and fell down the stairs. I know I've been a rotten cheat, but she nearly lost that baby, and I didn't realise how much they both meant to me until I saw her crying in the hospital because she thought she'd lost everything. I want to make it up to her. That's why I drove straight down. To ask you never to let her find out that I took you out those few times and that I asked you to...well, you know.' He looked shamefaced—utterly contrite, if that were possible, Fern thought with a mental grimace, numbed by what he had said. That a young woman was lying in hospital, thinking

her life in tatters, supposedly because of *her*, when all
her life she'd avoided married men like the plague. She
wanted to hit Greg, right between the eyes!

'I wasn't aware that there was anything to tell,' she
uttered disgustedly, wondering how long his intention to
reform would last. Somehow she doubted if men like
Greg Peters ever changed.

'Thanks. You're a great gal!' Relief was written all
over his face as he stood up, and before Fern had realised
what was happening his arms were around her and he
was murmuring into her hair, 'Thanks again,' just at the
moment that the door opened.

'Oh, hell!' Rooted to the spot by the accusation in
Connor's eyes, Fern heard Greg's agitated curse, his
laughed, embarrassed, 'Fern's just a friend. Tell him,
Fern,' before he made a hasty departure, leaving her to
face the chilling wrath of the older man alone.

'Yes, tell me, Fern,' Connor invited, with a frighteningly controlled anger, his teeth clamped so tightly
together that his words were almost a snarl. There was
a pallor to the skin stretched tight across his face, despite the deep Bermuda tan, and Fern took a step back,
feeling the tangible force of that controlled wrath licking
through his body beneath the casual elegance of his
clothes.

'You've got it wrong, Connor—again,' Fern emphasised despairingly, knowing from the look on his face
that it was useless even trying to explain. She'd wanted
to run into his arms the moment she saw him again; to
thank him for the T-shirt and pour out how much it had
meant to her. And now that innocuous little kiss from
Greg had ruined it all.

'Like hell!' he breathed, merely verifying her own
thinking, evoking a startled gasp from her as he threw
the door closed on the outer office. 'Just like I was wrong
when you suddenly switched off in Bermuda when his

father-in-law came on the line. I'm sick of your lies!' he
snarled roughly and, hitting his chin, 'I've had it up to
here! But I would have thought even you would have
some compunction about carrying on the affair while
his wife was lying in a hospital bed!'

'You don't understand,' Fern struggled to explain,
silently cursing Greg for turning up there, let alone
putting her in another compromising situation and then
just walking away to leave her to sort things out. Just
like last time, she thought, guessing that he probably
didn't even know how Connor had found her in his bed.
'He drove down here today to beg me not to tell Sarah,'
she gabbled, clutching the desk behind her to support
her unsteady legs, realising how attempts to absolve
herself were just making matters worse.

'I'll bet he did!' Connor's disgust was pulsing and
palpable. 'After all, if he loses Sarah, he loses a nice
prospective partnership in Harrison Stone with control
of the York office—a thing I'm sure he wouldn't want
to give up, even for you!'

It was no good, she thought desolately. There were
too many things against her; too deep a wound inside
him that made him judge her the same as the woman
who had hurt him so badly in the past. How he must
have loved his fiancée, to have been scarred so badly by
her! she thought, stabbed by his mistrust, a chill more
bitter than any she had known before creeping through
her as, in a voice as glacial as his eyes, he said simply,
'See you around, Fern.'

He had gone before she could utter a sound.

She didn't know how she got through the rest of the
day, hurting too much even to think beyond the merciful
demands of her job.

Fate had destroyed what chance of happiness she might
have had with Connor was all she could reason when
she was driving home that night, her tortured thoughts

and feelings flooding back with unbearable acuteness
now that she had emerged from the sheltering oblivion
of her work. The foolish hopes that he might have been
in love with her were blowing like torn curtains in the
wind, the reunion she had anticipated with such feverish
excitement and longing since she had come back from
Bermuda heralding only disaster when he had walked in
and found her in Greg's arms.

Oh, Connor! she sobbed silently, glad when at last she
was home, only to find that Queenie, laden with
shopping, was just coming in *and* in a chatty mood,
keeping her talking on the stairs for nearly an hour before
she could eventually get away.

When she was alone at last beneath the bedcovers,
convulsive sobs tore at her lungs so that she had to stifle
them in the pillow, craving only the painless oblivion of
sleep. But such sweet mercies eluded her, and eventually
she rose, looking pale and strained, and worrying, on
top of everything else, about her job.

Connor had threatened to tell Franklin about her in
the beginning when she'd tried to get out of going to
Bermuda with him. So would he tell the other man what
he had seen this time—witnessed in his friend's own
office while Franklin had been away?

She was on tenterhooks when her boss returned from
Yorkshire halfway through the morning, his beaming,
'Everything's going to be fine!' leaving her in no doubt
of the bond between the man and his daughter, and of
exactly what he would do if Connor disclosed what he
believed to be true.

Watering the plants in her employer's office, she wondered if she should tell him before Connor did—let him
know that she hadn't been a willing party to Greg's attempts to cheat on his wife. That way he could have
judged her by her own level of frankness before hearing
Connor's distorted version of the facts. But somehow

she couldn't bring herself to do it. In all probability
Franklin might not have the slightest inkling of what a
heel his son-in-law was, and there was no way she was
going to be the one to advise him—not because she had
any sympathy for Greg, but because of the dire consequences to which such a revelation could lead. There
was a woman's happiness at stake, a child's future. And
yet there was her own happiness, too—her job, hanging
in the balance...

One of the phones ringing on the desk broke into her
troubled thoughts, and she froze as she heard Franklin
greeting, 'Connor!' Fear made her throat contract as his
voice suddenly became more serious. 'I don't believe it!
When did you get to know about this...?'

So this was it, Fern thought, with a sickening ache in
her stomach, stealing quietly out of his office, back to
her own. The decision had been taken away from her,
she realised, anguished from Connor's brutal betrayal—
the knowledge that he could want to hurt her so much.

Agony tore across her heart, and blindly she began
pulling her personal belongings out of her desk—pens,
tissues, handcream—the pain unbearable, added to by
a deep regret, when Franklin eventually walked in.

'Having a clear-out?' Incredibly, his eyes were
twinkling! 'You can come and do mine next if you like.'

Fern stared at him, baffled. 'Wasn't that Connor on
the phone...?' Her stomach was still churning with the
prospect of being asked for her resignation, even when
Franklin gave a knowing chuckle.

'What were you hoping—that I'd put him on to you?
I'm not that stupid,' he grinned. 'The man's got enough
advantages over me without me letting him seduce my
best art director away, friend or no. He only stands to
make a few more million! Talk about the luck of the
devil! His top competitor's on the verge of liquidation
and is virtually begging him to buy them out.'

Dazed, disorientated, slowly Fern began to realise that that must have been what she had heard Franklin sounding so astounded by on the phone just now, and the pains in her stomach gradually began to ease. So Connor hadn't said a word about seeing her with Greg as she had so painfully imagined, and, now that she could reason beyond the realms of panic, her very instincts alone were enough to assure her that he would hardly be likely to. He might use his own strengths and powers to punish her, make her pay, but intuition told her that he would be as unwilling as she was to do anything that might have adverse effects on an already rocky marriage, and that she'd forgotten the integrity she'd been too ready to disregard.

Oh, *Connor*! she thought achingly, her heart overflowing with her futile love for him, so that it was only with an immense effort of will that she pulled herself together.

He still hated her, didn't he? And however *she* was feeling, the chances were *he* was feeling all right. He could never have loved her. And she could only assume now that, despite what he had said about wanting to trust her in Bermuda, he had never really believed her when she had told him about Greg. So she could only thank her lucky stars, she thought with a heart-scouring agony that in no way resembled gratitude, that she hadn't fully succumbed to that devastating sexuality.

The next couple of weeks passed with no further communication from him, and, to stop herself constantly thinking about him, Fern kept herself preoccupied with her work. She played hard too, filling her free lunch-hours with the occasional game of squash with one or two of her clients; going dancing with Jenny and some of the others from the office in the evenings, even managing the odd casual date. But the full, hectic days and sleepless nights were taking their toll of her appetite, as well as her sleep, so that even Franklin commented on her appearance when she walked into his office one morning.

'You've lost some weight, my lass, and it doesn't suit you. You look like a fashion-house mannequin—all severity and cheekbones and thin enough for a puff of wind to blow away. What does Connor think about it?'

He couldn't know how those innocuous words sent her heart ricocheting off her ribs. 'I haven't seen him.' With feigned nonchalance she pulled some dead flowers from a pink potted African violet, unaware of how her forced lightness brought his gaze skewering towards her, or of how keenly he was viewing her pale skin, touched pink where it stretched across the offending bones.

'Then we'll soon be rectifying that, lass. He's coming in this afternoon.'

Her body suddenly felt weak from more than just fatigue, each pulse point throbbing, her facial muscles aching from desperately trying not to give herself away.

'I'm sorry it's such short notice,' Franklin went on, 'but he rang yesterday wanting to know if the prints were ready. I didn't realise you had them yet, until I saw them on your desk last night. In fact, you've been sitting on this matter for nearly a week, Fern—that isn't like you. Connor might be a friend of mine, but he's still a darned calculating capitalist, as well as this company's biggest client. Delay his promotion campaign and I wouldn't blame him—in fact I'd expect it—if he took his business elsewhere!'

It was the closest thing Fern had had to a reprimand from her employer, and it wasn't pleasant, particularly as she knew she was guilty of not pulling out all the stops to get this meeting arranged. She had been busy in other areas, it was true, but she had put off phoning Connor to arrange for him to come in and select the prints for his brochure because she wasn't sure how she was going to face him when he did. Consequently it was with a sick, controlled nervousness that she attended the meeting at two-thirty prompt that afternoon.

Dressed in a dark suit, an immaculate white shirt emphasising the depth of his tan, he was standing near the window facing the door, and glanced up from saying something to Franklin as she entered, his gaze almost paralysing in its intensity.

'Fern,' he nodded, a gesture of cool detachment, though there was more than a casual interest in the way he surveyed her ultra-slim figure beneath the short-sleeved white blouse and tailored skirt.

'Hello, Connor. How have you been?'

Despite her thumping heart, she was pleased with how blasé she had managed to sound, though her teetering composure was tested as he sliced back, for her ears alone, 'Do you really want to know? Care?'

Nerves stretched to the limit, she couldn't think of anything to say, and she was relieved when Tony and Jenny, with Franklin's secretary, chose that moment to arrive, and their employer suggested they begin.

Somehow she found herself sitting at right-angles to Connor at the long table, the formal ambience of the consulting-room, broken only by a few luxuriant plants, conducive to the high-powered level of executive briefing with which he was clearly at home.

'Now what we have here, Connor, is a product of sheer genius.' Franklin was laying several of the prints down on the table and pushing them towards his client. 'I understand the two of you put your heads together on this one, and I must say you came up with something pretty impressive.'

It was a selection of the shots of Madree water-skiing with the parakite behind her, with some brilliant camera work on Tony's part capturing the exact effect that they had been hoping to achieve. But looking at Bermuda

again—the sun, the pink sand, that vivid blue ocean—
brought it all back, its warmth a palpable thing, and
Fern knew a swift longing to have things as they had
been between herself and Connor—the teasing, the
laughter, that first acknowledgement of her love for him
that had sung in her heart that day in that tiny zoo.

Nostrils flaring, greedy for even the smallest trace of
his scent, she looked up, across at him, recognising such
turbid emotion in his eyes that, heart-quickeningly, for
a moment, she thought he was remembering too. But
then his eyelids drooped, only a glacial composure remaining in the firm line of his mouth, cutting through
her as effectively as the stabbing familiarity of his
cologne.

'Mr McManus knew exactly what he wanted, so it was
just a matter of carrying out his instructions,' Fern responded, noting the barely discernible lift of his eyebrows at the way she had addressed him, while she
struggled to keep her own emotions well under control.
He couldn't know how much it hurt, sitting there going
through all this with him. And he wasn't going to find
out, she determined, flinching as she went to pick up
one of the prints at the same time as he was reaching
for his glass of water and his hand casually brushed hers.

'No. I merely added a final suggestion to something
that was already beyond *my* expertise.' It wasn't true,
that last bit, and Connor didn't have to praise her work.
Nevertheless, her blood still throbbed in her veins. 'No
wonder you wanted to hang on to them, Fern!' A tingling
heat stole through her as she realised he was speaking
to her. 'What were you planning to do—file them away
in your private album with all your other memories of
Bermuda?'

Fern's breath locked in her lungs. How could he be
so cruel? Franklin must have told him that she'd had

those prints for nearly a week—and he knew why, she thought, seeing the cool mockery in his eyes.

'I'm sorry you had to be kept waiting to see them,' she answered, desperate to stop him thinking the truth— that she couldn't face him—'but it really has been the most unbelievably hectic week. I must admit it was a temptation not to take them home with me...' For the sake of the others she tried to keep her tone light '...but you needn't have worried—glamorous though Bermuda was, it was all just in a day's work.'

She saw him frown—a movement of muscle that, like his silent enquiry just now, was scarcely detectable—but she ignored it, unable to look at him again because of the anguish his insensitivity had caused.

She was glad when the ordeal was over. She scooped up her folder as the meeting ended and uttered a polite, 'Good afternoon,' to him, but her heart sank when she heard Franklin call after her, detaining her from following Tony and the other two girls out of the room.

'I told you she was the best, didn't I?' Her boss was laughing loudly, slapping Connor's expensively jacketed shoulder. 'Stick with this young lady, lad, and I promise you'll never want for satisfaction.'

'Really?' Franklin's incautious remark had provided him with enough mocking innuendo to make her blush, though the amused curl of his lips didn't tally with the chilling beauty of his eyes. 'And do you think you can live up to Franklin's optimism, Fern?'

Tight-lipped, she responded with a private, sparring glance, panicking as she heard the phone ringing, then Franklin answering it, because it was some urgent message for her employer that, after a hasty, 'I'll be in touch,' to Connor, had him scuttling off.

'Well, I'm glad we've... *satisfied* you,' Fern said crisply, with deliberate emphasis, her heart pounding as she suddenly found herself alone with him. 'If you'd like to make an appointment to come in to discuss the media scheduling for the launching period...' with forced officiousness she was heading for the door '...I can see you one afternoon next week. Either Friday or——'

'Or what about having dinner with me this evening and we'll discuss it then?'

His startling suggestion brought her to a flabbergasted halt in the corridor. Desperately her eyes searched his for some flicker of emotion, but his face was like a cold, unreadable carving of marble.

'I'm sorry, I don't make a habit of accepting dinner invitations from clients,' she began, aching to accept but turning away, her features drawn, her blood racing, wincing sharply as he suddenly caught her by the arm.

'We aren't just talking about business here, and you know it!' he argued abrasively, and now she recognised a mutual tension graven on that harshly hewn face.

'Do I?' she parried, hurt and angry, her breasts lifting sharply beneath the prim white blouse. 'Why the sudden change of heart? Or do you want to blackmail me into something else? Because if so, Connor, I'm afraid those tactics really won't work on me any more. You can go ahead and tell Franklin what the hell you like. At least if he fires me, I won't have to deal with any more clients like you!'

'Fern!' His fingers tightened, bruising the softly tanned arm as she struggled for her freedom. 'If you want me to eat humble pie—all right, dammit, I will! I was wrong about you. I acted too hastily without even bothering to consider that you might be telling the truth——'

'But now you've had a chance to think about it you've decided I'm not such an out-and-out liar after all.' Her words ended almost on a sob, her senses reeling now from the numbing realisation that he did believe her—didn't hate her after all.

'Fern.' She couldn't resist as he turned her gently to face him, the dark eyes probing with such turbulent emotion into hers that she wondered if in fact it was really his pain she was seeing, or just a reflection of her own. 'I wanted to come round to your flat—call you. After that day I stormed out in such a rage—I was so desperate to see you again. But I was still angry too, even though I kept telling myself it didn't matter if you had twenty lovers, that I had to have you—all of you,' he breathed against the smooth skin of her temple, 'or lose my sanity. But you were right. I'd been hurt so much in the past that I couldn't bring myself to do it—couldn't climb down and swallow my pride and leave myself open to...' When he paused, she looked up at him enquiringly, seeing all the hurt he had harboured inside him because of that first cruel betrayal, and her heart lurched, swelling for him, growing with her love and her joy that he'd brought himself round to trusting her, believing her, judging her character on its own merits, giving her the benefit of the doubt.

'I was in a quandary for days about what to do. I wanted to see you—to hurt you—but I knew I'd only end up hurting myself in the process, and it wouldn't have done either of us any good, or made anything right. And then Greg came to see me and he told me everything, exactly as you had—that nothing had ever happened between you—except that he seemed to think your lack of interest was because of a passionless nature on your part.' He grimaced, clearly in wry dispute of that remark. 'But for all his sick pledges that he'd reformed, and his pleas never to tell Sarah, I as good as kicked him out. He's a jerk, and I strongly believe he'll never be anything else, but at least he...'

Fern wasn't listening to any more. Pain was suddenly clawing at her heart again, putting that tortured look back into her eyes. 'And yet you believed him?' she murmured with wounded incredulity. 'A rotten cheat like that—rather than me?' Hurting beyond hope, she pulled herself free from the torturing intimacy of his arms, her senses dangerously glutted with his scent, his voice, his warmth. 'Hadn't it ever occurred to you that a person needs to be trusted—believed for herself? Or does it take the lowest form of masculinity to convince you that there might be some good points in a woman after all?'

'Fern...'

'No!' she protested, panicking, side-stepping swiftly to avoid the treacherously sweet torture of his arms. 'You wouldn't listen to a word I said when you were accusing me of having an affair with Greg, but when the guilty party tells you there's nothing in it, because it's a man, it seems, then that's all right! Well, it isn't all right, Connor,' she advised him with the weight of her tears a trembling, choking sensation in her throat. 'How do you think it feels to know your suspicions about me were only allayed by a second-rate creep like that?'

'For heaven's sake, Fern! That wasn't the only——' Connor broke off as someone excused themselves to pass them, one of the new young directors, who viewed them with a polite smile that barely concealed his curiosity. 'That wasn't the only thing that got me thinking—of course it wasn't.' Connor's voice was thick with restraint as the other man disappeared into the consulting-room, yet Fern could sense the anger in him, see it in the dark glint in his eyes. 'Of course... it helped——'

'Naturally!' she snapped, lifting her head in a rebellious gesture so that the late afternoon sun shining through the long window at the end of the corridor fell across her fine features, making the stark, fragile bones stand out in proud relief. 'How do you know he wasn't lying, Connor, just to protect his own interests? No, you hadn't thought of that, had you?' she breathed, with the piercing intensity of a sword seeming to penetrate her heart when she saw the dark emotion that she could only deduce was uncertainty cross his face. 'In fact, why believe either of us?' Clumsily she went on, too hurt herself to fully appreciate what she was doing to him, 'After all, it's a more convincing admission isn't it? To confess to propositioning someone and being rejected rather than deny total participation in a full-blown, ongoing affair?'

A muscle pulled in the side of his jaw and his mouth was set in such grim lines that for a moment she thought, through her own abject misery, that he looked capable of physically abusing her. Well, let him, she accepted, feeling so desolate she really didn't care if he did, even as he said, in a voice that was quietly restrained, 'If you're trying to make me believe that then I'm afraid——'

'I wouldn't dream of it!' Fern retorted, her words poignant with wounded sarcasm. 'You wouldn't believe me if I told you night was dark or the earth was round, so I'm certainly not going to attempt to defend a simple thing like my character. You——'

'Fern! For heaven's sake, grow up!' The deep tones were suddenly sterner, impatient, making her flinch. He had said that once before, she remembered absently, aware of a telephone jangling along the corridor. 'I told you I was wrong. What more do you want me to do—write an epistle of undying contrition? I'm sorry, but humility was never my highest attribute. I apologise, profusely, but that's all I can do, Fern. You'll have to take it or leave it. It's entirely up to you.'

His eyes held hers, dark and inscrutable, the silence that stretched between them eternal. And then Franklin's colleague came out of the consulting-room, breaking the bubble of timelessness to announce, 'Telephone for you, Fern.'

She was scarcely conscious of her nodded acknowledgement, or of the man moving past them again. Her brain was in a whirlpool of confusion.

For a long moment they measured glances, while her heart cried that he couldn't do this to her! That he couldn't treat her so badly and then expect her to fall into his arms again, just like that, or terminate the relationship once and for all! But perhaps he could, she thought bleakly, guessing that he must have read that total hopelessness in her eyes, because suddenly his lips tightened and with an oddly bereft look he steeled himself as though to say something, but the next moment he had turned and was striding away.

CHAPTER ELEVEN

SCATTERING food into her fish tank, Fern watched one graceful shubunkin gently fanning the water over the coral Connor had given her, remembering that other aquarium and that sunbaked little zoo in Bermuda where she had first realised the depth of her love for him.

Remembering hurt—and it wasn't getting any easier, she thought torturedly, though it had been five weeks now since that last heartrending confrontation with him in the office.

He hadn't been into the agency, leaving the finalising of his company's promotion campaign to another member of his staff—a thing he had probably decided was for the best, Fern realised achingly, so that they wouldn't need to run into each other again.

Tears pricked her eyes as she tried to crush a continuing regret that she hadn't accepted him on his terms, rather than having to endure the chasm of emptiness she seemed to be living in now. But he had hurt her too much with his cruel accusations and suspicions—especially when it was only Greg's word he had believed—not trusting her enough to accept that she had moral standards of her own, listening to Greg who didn't have any at all. But if he couldn't trust her for herself, what hope would there have been for a future for them? logic forced her to reason with herself, and, even though she knew she had made the right decision, it didn't lessen the pain in any way, which made it torture being alone.

For that reason she decided to take a short break at the beginning of September, driving up to stay with her parents in their new Lakeland home.

'Good grief, Fern! You obviously aren't looking after yourself properly, are you?' Her mother's instant rebuke as Fern shrugged out of her light jacket was directed at her daughter's very evident loss of weight. 'You're as thin as a rake!'

Which was her mother's opinion of any woman who didn't top ten and a half stone! Fern thought wryly, as Janet Baxter was on the rather cuddly side. And even Fern's reminder that she took after her father for her slim build didn't stop a determined maternal, 'That's as may be! But while you're here with me, my girl, you're going to eat!'

Surprisingly, though, she did, finding a few days of brisk hillside walks restoring her appetite, while the long hours sailing with her parents in their small dinghy on the mountain-hemmed lakes put some bloom back into her cheeks. Their new house was lovely too—modern with scenic views, conducive to relaxation. Consequently, by the time she left she looked a little less fragile, less strained than the girl who had turned up on their doorstep five days before.

Being back in London with a weekend to face, however, wasn't a prospect Fern relished, because she knew a whole two days on her own would give her too much time to think. So when Saturday came and she noticed the fraying hem on the sports sweater she was rinsing out, she decided to make a special trip into town to treat herself to a new one.

Queenie was vacuuming the stairs as she came down, and commented on how pretty she looked in her white lacy top and jeans, going on to thank her for the shortcake Fern had brought her back from the Lake District for looking after her fish.

'Come down and have some when you've got a spare minute,' she invited, though from experience Fern knew she would need a spare couple of hours if she took up an invitation from Queenie. Appreciating, though, how lonely the little landlady must be and, nowadays, just how it felt, Fern smiled and promised that she would.

The trip into town was worthwhile. Choosing a sweater and some sweatbands in the first department store she tried, she was heading for the counter to pay for them when a heart-tugging, familiar figure at the check-out stopped her dead in her tracks.

Connor!

He looked devastating, a light shirt and hip-hugging brown cords complementing those tanned good looks. But it was the way he was looking down, saying something to the slender brunette beside him, that made Fern's heart twist painfully inside her.

Panicking, not wanting to be seen, she took refuge behind a macho-looking dummy stacked high with hiking equipment and peered through the gap under the dummy's arm.

With those Latin looks, this had to be Sabrina. The one who didn't make any demands on him! Fern remembered as pain ripped across her heart. She wasn't as olive-skinned as Fern had imagined, though that long, casually worn hair was easily as black as Connor's, and she was even lovelier than her name. Elegant too, even in a simple yellow blouse and pale cotton trousers, Fern noted, sick inside, wishing she could accuse her of looking like a stuck-up, supercilious snob—only she didn't. With that soft smile, the girl radiated a warmth which was probably why Connor liked her, it was torture to Fern to deduce. And they looked perfect together—a unit, she thought with a stabbing jealousy, the like of which she had never experienced before. And then the woman reached up and kissed him, a brief peck on the cheek, her face openly adoring before she walked away, leaving Connor pocketing his wallet and Fern feeling as if she had just witnessed her own execution.

Pain-stricken, she made to move off, hoping not to be seen. But he had turned—was looking in her direction! And swiftly she glanced down, assuming an interest in a pair of leather gloves that were lying on a glass stand, making up part of the display.

Dear heaven, don't let him see me! she pleaded silently, picking them up—and set a whole host of alarm bells into action.

Mortified, she could see the security wires now trailing from the gloves, cursing her own stupidity in touching the display. Also, because of the continuous, embarrassing clamour, people were stopping to look, and, red-faced, feeling like a shoplifter, Fern knew the wisest thing was to stay there until someone came to switch off the alarm, her plight soon bringing a female assistant scurrying over with a key at the same time as a deep voice behind her drawled, 'Well you really believe in drawing attention to yourself, don't you?' He stood looking mockingly down at her as the store was once again restored to merciful normality, while Fern blurted out her apologies to the now equally amused assistant.

'It's all right, madam, I can vouch for this woman's character,' Connor supplied jestingly, that incalculable charm evoking the dazzling type of smile to which he was obviously accustomed before the girl, having repositioned the gloves, left the two of them alone.

'Thanks,' Fern offered pithily, not sure whether it was the embarrassment of setting off the alarm or coming face to face with Connor that had started her trembling. 'Why didn't you add that I don't steal anything except other people's husbands?'

He made a wry movement with his mouth and said drily, 'Because you can't get locked up for that.'

Fern caught her breath. Did he still doubt her innocence, then? She would never know. And anyway, it didn't really matter now, did it?

'What were you doing looking at a pair of men's designer gloves? Sending someone off mountain climbing?' Amusement was threaded through the silky-smooth timbre of his voice. 'Or were they a secondary issue to something more interesting on this floor?'

He'd seen her? Been aware of her peering round the dummy, watching them both? Him and Sabrina and that intimate, heart-lacerating kiss!

'I thought they'd make a nice present for someone.' The blatant lie sprang to her lips, coming easily, desperate as she was to conceal the truth—the agony of her painful, hopeless love for him.

An eyebrow arched as he stooped to turn over the price tag. 'At——?' He quoted the cost, grimacing. 'Is he that special?' he asked, his sceptical tones assuring her he didn't believe it for one minute.

Fern bit her lip nervously, bringing her head up in a rebellious cloud of gold. Connor could see through her thin charade. And perhaps he could see something else too, mirrored in the agony of her face, she thought wretchedly, because his fingers touched her arm, sending a torrent of remorseless sensation through her as he said softly, 'You're still shaking. Come on, I'll buy you a coffee.'

She wanted to refuse, but she couldn't, wanting—needing him—craving to be with him in any way she could. Numbly she was aware of him relieving her of the goods she had been about to buy, discarding them on a counter they were passing, feeling his hand at her elbow as she allowed him to guide her through the congested store.

As they came out of the lift on the lower level, she noticed the swimwear sale, evidence that the holiday season was drawing to its close. The brightly coloured shorts and bikinis reminded her of Bermuda, but she didn't want to think about that, her tortured brain grasping at numb reality, the peal of till registers, the loud confusion of conversations, the cloying scent of some new fragrance being promoted near one of the perfume counters.

'Here, sit here.'

Hardly aware of it, she found herself hustled into the store's crowded coffee-shop, collapsing on to the chair Connor pulled out for her before he shot off to join the queue at the self-service counter.

She was feeling more relaxed when he returned with the coffee, and as he sat down opposite her she said with the slightest tremor, 'You're looking well.'

It wasn't strictly true. There were signs of tiredness about his beautiful eyes and mouth, as if he had been working too hard, and she paid for her nervous little fib when he returned with uncomplimentary succinctness, 'You're not.' His grim regard of her was as merciless as paint stripper, burning into the layers of her invisible, shell-thin immunity to him. Colour winged its way up her throat and across her cheeks and her gaze faltered beneath such intense discernment as quietly, his tone edged with a bitter-sweet sensuality, he murmured, 'Missing me, Fern?'

Her lashes shot upwards, unwittingly revealing the clouded misery in her eyes. How dared he? After the way she'd seen him with that other woman! But she said calmly enough, 'What on earth gave you that idea?'

'You.' Against the other sounds in the restaurant, his voice seemed softly amused, although as his eyes raked over the gaunt lines of her face she sensed an uncharacteristic tenseness about him too. 'You look tired, far too thin—as if you've been starving yourself. And you've been stirring your coffee for the last thirty seconds, though you haven't even put any sugar in it yet.'

Naturally he would notice that! Flustered, Fern reached for the sugar bowl, giving a little gasp as a strong hand came down over hers.

Oh, God, how she'd longed for his touch! Her gaze darted from their two hands, hers pale gold against his bronze, to his face, her eyes wide and panicking, and something like a live current ran through her when he breathed, 'It's entirely mutual, Fern.'

Excitement coursed through her blood, her pulse throbbed beneath the firm pressure of his thumb, and her heart felt as if it were going to beat itself right out of her chest.

'Something happened to me in Bermuda that I wasn't prepared for—didn't want to happen. But it did, and now I find I can't sleep at night—can't stop thinking about...well, what we could be doing together, unless I drive myself non-stop into my work—try and drive that lovely face of yours out of my mind. I want you, Fern, as I've never wanted any woman in my life.'

His ragged declaration brought a yearning response singing through her veins. Was he saying he loved her? No, not that, she assured herself achingly, a sick, cold pain striking at her heart, the strain accentuated in her face as she recalled the scene she had witnessed upstairs.

'No,' was all she could manage to protest feebly, trying to free her hand, but Connor caught her other one as well, refusing to let her go.

'Yes,' he breathed, and with such determination that a small *frisson* ran through her with a little tingle of fear. Fear of her own vulnerability.

He didn't love her. The way he'd looked at that other woman up in the sports department, that was love, the deep affection she wanted from him, along with his deep, undying trust. But of course he didn't trust her either.

He was too ready always to believe the worst about her. Even when Greg had told him the truth, he'd found it too easy to resurrect those doubts about her when she had stupidly suggested that Greg might have been lying for his own ends. She'd seen the uncertainty so clearly in his eyes. And because he didn't believe her, neither could he respect her, which was why he thought she would simply jump into bed with him regardless of any commitments on his part—or probably on hers—because she was that type of girl, easy and unprincipled, not worried about who else might possibly get hurt.

'And what about your girlfriend?' She jerked a glance towards the ceiling. 'Sabrina?' Her heart was pounding, her stomach queasy from having to acknowledge that she'd seen them together. 'Don't you care what she's going to think about it? Or is she just another woman—like me—incapable of engendering any trust?'

Connor's fingers tightened on hers, then relaxed, although his jaw seemed rigid with tension and there was a dark glint of something in his eyes.

'You really know how to try a man's patience, don't you?' he rasped with a deep expansion of his chest. 'And either I've been rather remiss in the whole darn process of communication with you, or rather stupid—but you've got yourself in one hell of a twist, lady!'

'Have I?'

'Yes!' There was an angry flush beneath his tan. 'Just because you witnessed an innocent kiss between myself and some woman I happen to be with——'

'Innocent?' Fern retorted scathingly. 'Good grief, you just have to look at her to know she's crazy about you!'

'I don't dispute it.' His mouth quirked. 'And the feeling's entirely reciprocal. I've known her a long time. She——'

He broke off as Fern jumped up, knocking the table and spilling coffee on to the smooth veneer.

'I don't want to hear your explanations,' she said
brittly, an agony of emotion on her face. 'Thanks for
the coffee, Connor, but I'm not thirsty.' Her only thought
was to get away, but before she could he had reached
across the table, catching her by the wrist.

'Look, we've got a lot of talking out to do—and a
crowded coffee-shop isn't the place to do it.' He glanced
impatiently towards a neighbouring table whose occu-
pants were already looking interestedly their way. 'Come
with me back to the car——'

'No!' Her swift, alarmed objection sprang from an
overpowering longing to go with him, but she knew that
if she did—if he got her alone—he could make her agree
to anything, without principle, without commitment,
without trust.

'For heaven's sake, Fern! If you don't want to make
a complete spectacle of us both, sit down, because I
shan't let you go until you do!'

She stopped resisting him instantly, doing as he said,
and he took a short, sharp breath, withdrawing his hand.

'I don't really think any girlfriend of mine is the real
issue here, and you're just dying for me to say it, aren't
you? Well, all right. So let's get what we're thinking off
our chests! Personally I think you could do with a few
lessons in the art of listening, and I'm in no doubt at
all what you're thinking about me. You're sure I must
be wondering why a girl who's supposed to be so sophisticated, with no real aversion to splitting up a marriage,
will let a little thing like a . . . live-in girlfriend pose any
problem. So why does it, if you can be involved with
Greg and if, without sounding too conceited, you want
me more than I think you ever wanted him? Why should
it matter, Fern?'

Cruel talons of ice seemed to be tearing at her heart
as her eyes searched the dark, inscrutable depths of his.
He looked oddly strained from an emotion she could

only guess was his basic, consuming need of her, and she tried to speak but couldn't, her breath dragging through her lungs, crushed by the brutally casual way he had just admitted to living with Sabrina and to wanting *her* as well.

Humiliatingly, she felt the give-away trembling of her lower lip, the bite of tears behind her eyes, and, jumping up, in a strangled whisper she was murmuring, ''Bye, Connor,' then darting away before he could see how much his verbal cruelty was destroying her.

Over all the other sounds in the café she thought she heard him call her name, but she was running blindly out of the store and into the street, to lose herself completely in the merciful crowds.

The following days were something simply to get through, with no further word from Connor, until one morning Franklin called Fern into his office.

'Connor wants this...' he held up a finished copy of ALI's brochure, fresh from the printers '...dropped in to him tonight. I was doing it on my way home, but unfortunately I've got a meeting at the other end of town and can't get it to him, so I've told him you'd drop it off as it's on your way.'

Fern's stomach muscles contracted into a tight knot. He couldn't ask her to do this—he couldn't! 'Isn't there anyone else who could take it?' she ventured. Then, realising how uncooperative that sounded, 'I mean... I'll do it if there's absolutely no one else, but I wasn't thinking of going straight home...'

She hated lying, but she didn't know how she could face Connor again, especially somewhere so personal as his flat—the very place where he had first accused her of having illicit relations with Greg. But her stomach turned over as Franklin replied in abnormally uncompromising tones, 'There's positively no one else.'

She couldn't concentrate on a thing after that, and spent the rest of the day wondering how she was ever going to appear calm in front of Connor when she was dying inside.

A phone call from him later that afternoon started her blood gushing, though the initial surge of anticipation and hope that ran through her on hearing his voice was quickly quashed when he made no reference to the conversation they'd had in the restaurant—or even his wanting to see her again, the uppermost factor in his mind his company's advertising.

'I understand you're dropping by with the brochure.' His voice was cold and impersonal. 'I've got to go up to town and shan't be here, but Sabrina will be.' And on a more patronising note, 'Don't ram it through the letterbox, will you, Fern?'

He had done it deliberately, just to hear her reaction, she decided, her torment excruciating, threatening to betray her as she clung on to her composure long enough for him to ring off.

How *could* he? Vicious spasms of anguish tore through her body. Not only was he enjoying flaunting his precious Sabrina in front of her, he was even subjecting her to a meeting with the woman, only guessing perhaps at a fraction of the turmoil she would suffer because of it. And why? To make her suffer for being the type of girl he thought she was?

She left her office that evening with a resigned, chilling emptiness and a gnawing tension deep in the pit of her stomach.

'Fern?' Franklin called out to her as she was passing his door, and, looking in, she saw him holding up a key. 'No one's going to be in at Connor's, so you'll need this, lass. Let yourself in and leave that brochure on the lounge table with the key.' And, seeing the bewilderment on her face, 'There won't be anybody there,' he re-iterated impatiently, as if she was some halfwit.

And that was precisely how she felt, she realised, with an aching relief trickling through her blood. Had the woman changed her mind about waiting in for her? Or had Connor simply been saying she'd be there just to hurt her—just to make her extremely unhappy for a few hours? Also, how did Franklin come to have the key?

She was tussling with emotion as she started her car and drove out to the expensive suburb, and her insides knotted up when she got out and walked up to that familiar front door.

Without really knowing why, she rang the brass bell, just to be sure, and surprise broke through her tension when a dog started barking somewhere inside the flat.

Did Connor own a dog? A picture of some monstrous creature with snarling teeth flashed through her mind, the excited barking from just behind the door now making her fear, when there was no answer to her ring, if it was safe to go inside.

Gingerly, heart pounding with apprehension, she eased the door ajar, her tentative, 'Easy, boy, easy!' needless when she was suddenly besieged by a friendly, leaping retriever, pale gold and boisterous, her face a target for a warm, wet canine tongue.

'I could be a burglar and you'd still lick my hand, wouldn't you, boy?' Fern couldn't help laughing. Then, realising her mistake, 'Sorry, girl!' she corrected with a little grimace. She hadn't imagined Connor keeping an animal, let alone such a gentle-hearted one!

Patting the soft, warm head, she went through into the lounge, trying not to remember the last time she had been there, that unpleasant episode with Greg, her migraine, meeting Connor...

Her heart was a lead weight inside her as she put the large brown envelope and key on the glass coffee table as instructed, then crouched down to pet the dog that had followed her in.

'What do they call you, girl?' She caught the little round silver tag attached to the blue tartan collar, laughingly dodging the dog's attentions to read it.

It was twisted round, reverse side up, showing Connor's name with the address and telephone number of the flat. Fern turned it over. Saw the name 'Honey' engraved in brackets, and above it, the stronger, bolder characters, 'SABRINA BIANCA'.

CHAPTER TWELVE

'*YOU'RE* Sabrin...' Her shocked words tailed away, her brain struggling to understand. All along she had assumed that Sabrina was Connor's girlfriend, and not once had Connor put her straight. And all the time it was the pedigree name of a dog!

'Well, I expected a bitch, but not the furred variety!' she expressed on a burst of tight laughter strung with irony and self-derision, and, uncontrolled, a furore of emotion brought her head down against the animal's warm coat, her tears suddenly turning into convulsive, suffocating sobs, dampening the silky, doggy-smelling fur.

'Oh, God, what an idiot I've been!' she groaned when she could control herself enough to start reasoning again. But why had he let her go on thinking it—making a fool of herself?

Laughing, crying, half angrily she brushed at her wet cheeks, angry with herself for her utterly juvenile stupidity. Connor must have been laughing at her all along—and it served her right! she castigated herself as she sobbed laughingly down at the grinning retriever and remembered what he had said out there in Bermuda about Sabrina making no claims on him.

And the woman in that store? Who was she? she started wondering, then dismissed her as insignificant. What did it matter? She wasn't Sabrina. Sabrina whom she had thought Connor was seriously involved with. Whom Franklin had referred to that first day as the lovely lady in Connor's life! Good grief, he must have been laughing up his sleeve every time she'd accused him of cheating on his dog! So why hadn't he told her the truth?

Struggling to her feet, she knew she had to get out of there. She was much too vulnerable where he was concerned—and she needed time to think. If she didn't, and he came back and saw that she'd been crying, he'd know then how much she loved him, and although she knew now that Sabrina wasn't a threat to her—understood, too, how intensely Connor wanted her—it was only a physical wanting. He didn't love her. He didn't trust her enough for that.

Honey sprang ahead of her as she came into the wide hallway, but when Fern went to open the door, the dog's lip curled back with a low, throaty growl.

'It's all right, Honey, I'm not——' She broke off, surprised as a second attempt to let herself out was impeded by another, more ferocious sound, and Fern stepped back, alarmed, her face turning ashen. How could an animal so amiable and gentle one minute turn into six stone of snarling animosity the next? 'Good girl. Good dog.' Cautiously she tried again, but Honey was having none of it, jumping up and grabbing her sleeve with such a fierce yelp that quickly, fearfully, Fern retracted her hand, admitting with a bitter irony that Connor had had the last laugh on her again. So much for assuming he'd have a dog that would be anything but useful to him! Anyone who got in here might get her hand licked, but it would be as good as bitten off when she tried to get out!

Going back into the lounge, she sat down on the settee, the ugly memory of Greg throwing those banknotes down when she'd refused to get involved with him sending a violent shudder through her body. The situation had been as distasteful to her as any she could have imagined, and yet Connor had thought—still believed—she could be a party to such abhorrent behaviour!

The sound of the dog padding in dragged her mind back to the present, and she shrank back against the settee as it came and sat down in front of her, then, amazingly, started pawing at her skirt.

'So you've decided I'm all right, have you?' Fern reproved, breathing again, tentatively putting out a hand and finding, surprisingly, that the dog allowed her to stroke its soft, warm muzzle. 'Well, I'm sorry, but I'm not staying here and playing games with you all night,' she scolded gently, and got up, only to discover, at the front door again, that Honey had other ideas. This time when she tried to open it, the dog jumped up to catch her sleeve—and with such a determined snarl that, terrified, Fern dropped her bag and keys and tore back into the lounge, having to accept that she was utterly trapped.

Damn Connor! Discarding her jacket, she went over to the cocktail cabinet and, knowing she would need all the courage she could muster to help her through the ordeal of meeting him again, poured herself a large Martini, glass knocking nervously against glass. So at least she looked relaxed, sitting there with one of his marine magazines open on her lap, when he came in, though her pulse was racing like mad.

Casually dressed, he oozed a raw, male vitality that took her breath away as he smiled, having the nerve to inject surprise into the way he remarked, 'Are you still here?'

Resenting the way he could still turn her legs to jelly after he'd had the audacity to trap her there, Fern returned stiffly, 'Surprise, surprise! *Sabrina* wouldn't let me out.'

'Ah, so you've met?' He was fondling the dog as it jumped up at him excitedly, the movement of black hair falling across his brow causing Fern's heart to lurch. 'Good girl! You did a great job.'

'A great job!' Fern closed the magazine she had been reading and tossed it down on the coffee-table, her eyes following him accusingly as he straightened and with a casual, relaxed grace, removed his jacket, discarding it over a chair. 'That was a dirty rotten trick! I could have been savaged,' she said more defensively, dragging her gaze from the play of those muscles beneath the fine shirt, the aching familiarity of the way he moved, the way he held his head, too poignant to bear.

One easy movement brought him down beside her and her throat seemed to clog as his arm came to rest behind her across the back of the settee.

'I promise you she'd never savage anyone.' It was a simple enough statement, but his voice was too warm, too velvety, much, much too sensual. Fern watched the hand that was playing carelessly with one long, silken canine ear, noticed how the dog looked up at him with dark, rapturous eyes, utterly smitten. As she was, Fern thought despairingly.

'That's not the point,' she complained, a quiver in her voice from the heady effect Connor's proximity and that lethal magnetism was having on her weak, assailable femininity. 'Do you usually resort to kidnapping when a woman doesn't want to see you any more?'

He smiled. 'Oh, but this one does.'

Her breath was a rush of air through her lungs as she felt the warmth of his palm against her cheek, recognising the mutual wanting in those oddly tumultuous brown eyes. He was hypnotising her, she thought dizzily, feeling her body grow weak, barely conscious of the muted sound of traffic in the street outside, the faint whirr of the video recorder in the corner of the room, the dog's quiet breathing, desire trickling through her like a viper's deadly poison, paralysing her reasoning powers and her will. She wanted him now, whatever painful consequences she might have to face in the future—and they would be painful, she assured herself with bitter acknowledgement, because of his inability to trust. Yet, not caring, loving him too much to listen to logic, she strained towards him, her face an open message of need and wanting and desire. But he held her away from him and got up, saying coolly, apparently without any of the emotion that was consuming her, 'Besides, it was the only way I could keep you here long enough to listen to what I had to say.'

'Which was...' she couldn't help it, frustration urging her to supply ' ... that you want me whether or not I've had twenty lovers and even if I am still involved with Greg?'

'Yes.' He breathed the word harshly through his teeth, his face dark and rigid with something suppressed, bringing Fern's lashes down in painful acceptance of just what he thought about her—would always think of her. And, because she was like that, she wasn't really sure what happened next, but suddenly he was dragging her up from the settee, his torn, 'For God's sake!' an angry admonition as he pulled her roughly against him, his hands imprinting their bruising possession on her arms. 'When are you going to stop reminding me of how wrong I was about you? Or are you getting some kick out of continually torturing me for my stupid folly. For heaven's sake, can't you give me—*us*—a chance?'

She couldn't believe the raw emotion in him. Dancing with hope, her eyes searched his, half afraid to acknowledge what they saw there, even while her brain tried to grasp what he had just said. Hazily she was aware of Honey on her feet again, running excitedly around them.

'I know it was wrong of me to instantly think you'd been lying to me when I saw you in Greg's arms that day, but the evidence seemed pretty damning, and I think anyone would have done the same in the circumstances. But I've already admitted that you were right—I was being influenced by things that had happened in the past. I liked to think I was strong enough not to let them affect me, but I'm not that superhuman, although I was telling you the truth—or tried to—when I said that I'd already made up my mind about you before Greg even came to see me. The girl I cared for before—or thought I did——' he grimaced, his expression remote as he looked back to some other time into which she couldn't follow '—had no scruples, no sense of humour, nor that childlike love of nature that you have. I knew you could never be like her. You drive me crazy as she never did, but I was as scared as hell to admit it consciously to myself because I was in so deep with you. Apart from which, it takes a lot, admitting one's been wrong, particularly to oneself. When I told you that day, though, in the office, you seemed to make me want to believe all the things I'd convinced myself you weren't, and it wasn't that I believed them—just that I couldn't understand why you were trying so hard to convince me they were true—as though you wanted us to break up.'

'Because I thought you were ready to take Greg's word when you wouldn't believe mine...' murmured Fern, breathless from his statement a moment ago about being in so deep with her. What did he mean? In love? '...even if it did amount to the same thing.'

'But you wouldn't listen when I tried to tell you that it wasn't only that. You wouldn't listen to me when I tried to talk to you in that coffee-shop the other——'

'Because you were trying to make me think——'

'There you go again!' His voice was a soft reprimand as he gently gathered her into his arms. 'I'm going to have to do something about that.'

'Like what?' she challenged tremulously, quivering with sensation when he laughed softly and bent his head to nibble the sensitive skin beneath the collar of her blouse. 'You tried to make me think Sabrina was your girlfriend!' she reminded him hotly, trying to push away from him, her voice unintentionally conveying all the anguish she had known from imagining him with her. Her. The woman she had seen him with in that store.

'You made yourself think that,' he corrected her quietly. 'And when you had the nerve to tell me you never jumped to conclusions, and were so downright cocksure about it, I——'

'So that was why...!' Fern broke off, remembering just how cocky she had been about that when she had been accusing him of the same thing, wondering what he must have thought, her expression suddenly sheepish, both from that and the tender reproof in his eyes for interrupting him yet again. 'But you still led me on to think she was someone you were involved with, by what you said in that store—and today on the phone...'

Wounded bewilderment tinged her words as she tried to comprehend his actions, and her mind and body ached for him as he drew her back to him, so close she could feel the heavy beating of his heart.

'Not today. I merely said Sabrina would be here— which was the truth. But yes, I admit, the other day I did want you to think it—but only to assess your reaction. To find out once and for all exactly how you felt. I couldn't have hurt you more if I'd mortally wounded you—I could see that much before you ran away from me, and it stabbed me like hell, but I must confess to feeling extremely exuberant as well, because it showed me how you felt about me, and I knew that if I could get you here...'

'I wouldn't stand a chance?' Her words were softly admonishing, but her face was glowing with a radiant youthfulness as Connor bent his head to kiss her lightly on her nose.

'Precisely.' He sounded pleased with himself, his lips moving, feather-light, across hers. 'I wasn't sure how I was going to do it until I called in to see Franklin the other day, and when he mentioned the brochure being ready in a day or two it presented me with the golden opportunity I was looking for. I gave him a key and told him to send you round with it and that if you tried to wriggle out of it, as I guessed you probably would, to use his authoritative powers any way he could to ensure you came—without letting on that I wanted you here. He was very obliging...' his mouth pulled with undisguised smugness '...after he'd called me a few choice names and told me to leave you with enough energy to keep his office running efficiently.'

And between two such clever, conniving brains, Fern thought, blushing from the implication of Connor's last words, she hadn't had a hope of getting out of doing exactly what he had planned.

His lips had found their way to the sensitive, beating hollow at the base of her throat, but with a delicious little shiver she held him back, a tiny crease between her brows.

'So who was that woman I saw you with?' she demanded in mock accusation. 'Was she the "something more principled" you were expecting that Sunday when you were so keen to get me home?'

Connor laughed at the small, jaundiced note she had been unable to keep out of her voice. 'I'm afraid I was referring to Honey,' he explained with a self-recriminating grimace, reminding her of just how disparaging his opinion of her had been. 'But if you hadn't interrupted me and jumped to all the wrong conclusions when I was trying to explain last week, you'd have known who I was with.' And with a mischievous glint in his eyes, 'That was Helen—my sister,' he enlightened her. 'She wanted me with her to help her choose some new golf clubs for Dad's birthday—as well as to foot half the bill! But when you were quite determined she was Sabrina, I decided it was about time you met this adoring creature you'd dreamed up for me who was so indulgent towards the other women in my life.' Fern followed his gaze to the dog sitting, head cocked, watching them with large knowing eyes. 'As well as being extremely intelligent, eh, girl?' Honey gave a low whine of anticipation—captivated, just as she was, Fern thought resignedly, by the deep, warm velvet of her master's voice. 'Do you know, she even had a place for you at Cambridge?' he told the dog, his laughing remark bringing a small, ineffectual fist into playful contact with his arm.

'Well, you said about dropping her off at the college...' Fern explained in an emphatic attempt to save face, remembering his conversation with Franklin at that lunch that day and seeing now the reason for that private joke about Sabrina getting her degree.

'When I go away Helen always looks after her, but she lives in Surrey, and sometimes it's easier to drop her off at the college where my brother-in-law lectures—then he takes her home with him in the evening.'

'You...!' Another light thump, this time on his chest, accompanied her laughing admonition, then the soft sound turned to a sensual little gasp as he caught her hard to him, his mouth on hers turning fun into fervour, playfulness to passion, desire a mutual hunger that demanded only to be sated as she gloried in his hard embrace.

There were no words between them now; passion dominated, as their lips and hands sought each other in a furnace of blinding, driving need, a desperate, breathless urgency to remove the barriers of clothing that separated them, so that, with garments strewn across the lounge floor, somehow they wound up in Connor's bed.

Their wanting was too great for any large degree of petting; their bodies were impatient, demanding only total unity with the other.

When Connor took her Fern cried out, but from the unimagined pleasure of his engulfing strength and power, engulfing him in turn in her own softness, feeling his need, fierce and yet surprisingly controlled, as if he'd realised—or perhaps even remembered—her lack of experience as he took her with him over the brink, into a gasping, sobbing abyss of sensation, making her a woman, making her whole—wholly his.

She was damp with sweat, luxuriating in a sweet, sensual lassitude, her head against the warm, musky cushion of Connor's shoulder. He stirred, his lips caressing her hairline, and she uttered a small sound of contentment and turned towards him, the desire she had thought sated a twinge of familiar hunger deep in her loins.

'You're insatiable,' he whispered, raising himself up on his elbows and smiling down at the slumbrous desire in her young face. 'You know, I must confess I planned this moment from that first night I came in and saw you lying here . . . to get you back here in my bed. It was all I could think about.' His fingers were teasing a tendril of blonde hair that was curling against her temple, caressing the damp satin of her cheek, her throat, finding the silken valley between her breasts. 'What I wasn't planning was any long-term relationship, though . . . with anyone . . .'

Lids heavy, mouth like chiselled rock, Fern couldn't tell what he was really thinking, and her eyes clouded with uncertainty. Of course, he hadn't said he loved her, and she'd known that if she stayed she would accept him on any terms, and he'd known that too.

He was leaning across to the bedside cabinet, taking something out of the drawer. It was the necklace she had left with him to return to Ross before she had flown home.

'I tried to give it back to him,' he explained in answer to her baffled surprise, 'but you know Ross. He asked me—was hoping I could give it to you as his wedding present,' he stated drily, then, 'probably guessing how much I wanted you, but for . . . reasons of my own I couldn't do that. It wouldn't have been . . . ethical,' he added, and she knew why he hesitated. Because he didn't want her as his wife? Just to be her lover? A cold chasm of emptiness was suddenly widening inside her. So why couldn't she be content with that? 'I knew you probably wouldn't be that happy accepting it from him anyway, so I offered him its market value, but he wouldn't take that either, although in the end I had no trouble interesting him in one of the new toys out of the latest brochure. So now he's happy with the newest innovation on water, and this...' he was unfastening the necklace '...is bought and paid for...' lashes lowered, his gaze burned with an incandescent fervour over her body '...just like you.'

The necklace was a shock of cold sensuality against her heated skin, yet the implication of those last words sent a small wounding dart arrowing through her. Was he making a point, because of what she'd said in the beginning about him not being able to afford her? she wondered sadly, her hands going up to the catch in protest as she heard it snap firmly in place.

'Keep it on.'

When Ross had said that to her it had been more as a plea, but from Connor it was a definite order, and one that sent a sharp *frisson* through her despite a reluctance to accept such obvious domination and her wounded suspicions that he thought she needed to be bought.

She caught her breath as he suddenly tugged the duvet back so that he could appreciate her body fully, sensation a traitor as she felt his dark regard moving over her, saw the flush of passion in his face, the sensual smile that curved his lips, bringing her tongue tentatively across her own.

'You look thoroughly...debauched,' he said.

'So why did you buy it for me? Expect me to wear it?' she murmured in wounded puzzlement, recognising an almost feral satisfaction in his eyes. Her breasts lifted, perfectly rounded, their darker, swelling aureoles thrust upwards in unwitting enticement as she tried again to deal with the stubborn clasp.

'I don't—not in public, anyway,' he told her, pulling a wry face, drawing a trembling throaty sound from her as his hands suddenly came up to accept the tantalising invitation of her breasts. 'But it has its uses.'

Yes, like turning him on! she thought, gasping in sudden realisation of his arousal, his hardening body thrilling—exciting her.

She sighed her pleasure from the warm caress of his hands on the outer curves of her breasts, her body jerking in a spasm against his hard warmth as he drew one sensitive nipple into his mouth and then the other, his teeth tugging on their tender tips until she was writhing in a sobbing, mindless frenzy of desire, ready to do anything he asked.

He knew what he was doing, she thought hazily, through the dizzying ecstasy of this love game he was playing with her, because she *felt* debauched—as wanton and debauched as he'd said she looked, moving convulsively beneath him and the heavy gold chain that adorned her slim, agile body, glorying in the heightened sensuality it gave to her throbbing, tumescent breasts, her creamy nakedness and the darker, downy triangle of her femininity.

Wanton and uninhibited, she allowed her instincts to guide her, pleasing him, then, without any reservation, following as he led her, exploring the dark velvet of his skin with her lips and hands and tongue, feeling his body grow taut beneath her unrestrained caresses, learning from the wealth of his expertise.

This time when he entered her there was no holding back, and she wanted none, her hips rising to meet the hard thrust of his body with a riding urgency of their own. She felt the hot white tide of fire start to tingle along her thighs, spreading outwards from the very core of her being, and a sobbing gasp was torn from her throat simultaneously with Connor's deep groan of release, and joyously now she accepted the climax of his fierce possession in the sudden flow of life-milk that ebbed from his body into hers.

She must have slept then, serene and fulfilled, waking to the sound of his deep, regular breathing and a few small anxieties. For instance—was she pregnant? And if she was, would it please him? Make him happy? Because to have his child, she realised suddenly, was the thing she wanted most in the whole world.

Connor moved, breathing a long, shuddering sigh—in sleep, she thought, until he spoke.

'Marry me.' It was a desperately raw command against the soft translucency of her cheek and she tilted her head to look up at him, her heart aching from the depth of emotion she saw in him, the vulnerability in every taut line and contour of his face.

'Why?' she whispered, her heart suddenly as light as air, the realisation that he was asking her to stay, to live with him for a lifetime, bringing tears bubbling up inside her so that she hid them behind a shaky little laugh. 'So I can look after your dog?'

'Answer me.' His voice was rough as he pulled her round under him again, the agony of suspense she read in his dark, searching eyes piercing her to the quick.

'Yes, yes,' she murmured against his lips. 'Yes!' her blood singing with the knowledge that he cared, more than she had ever hoped, and with the staggering re-alisation suddenly of the phenomenal amount he must have paid in real terms—and over the odds—for what was really no more to him than a love-toy! Fern gave a little giggle in her throat, fingering the necklace with a tingling pleasure. Life with Connor McManus was never going to be dull!

*   *   *

It was Honey, nosing Connor's shoulder, who finally
stirred them from the warm aftermath of their love-
making, her soft whines eventually getting them up.

'I think she's feeling neglected,' he laughed, when they
had showered and dressed and the dog was still voicing
her protest at the two of them standing, sharing kisses
over coffee in the large, lived-in kitchen. 'She's long
overdue for her walk.'

'Oh, dear, and after she did such a great job for her
master too!' Fern laughed with meaning, tugging out of
his arms with a squeal when she realised his playful, lip-
tightening purpose to turn her over his knee. 'How did
you manage to train a dog like that to hold people here,
anyway?'

'I didn't,' he said laconically, putting an arm about
her shoulders, a click of his tongue sending Honey
leaping off through the flat with an ecstatic yelp as they
made their way to the front door. 'You could easily have
got out.' And with a jerk of his chin, 'Go on,' he said,
holding back for her to precede him along the passageway. 'Try opening the door.'

Fern looked at him dubiously, glancing at the bundle
of honey-blonde fur that was waiting eagerly beside it,
then doing as he said.

'See!' she breathed, jumping back, startled, as the dog
leaped up at her again, tugging at her sleeve. And, rather
worriedly, 'I don't think she really likes me at all.'

She couldn't understand why Connor was grinning.

'Nonsense,' he said. 'She likes everybody. She knows
you're going out and wants to go with you, that's all.'
He was still smiling as he came along the passageway,
indicating a leash that was hanging behind the door, advising gently, 'Pick it up.'

Fern frowned uncertainly, but complied, then gave a
little gasp of laughter when, on trying the door this time,

she found no opposition, and the dog shot out, bounding happily down the path.

'Talk about collusion!' she scolded lightly, with the late evening sun streaking amber through her hair as she met the laughter in that strong, adorable face. 'And you knew I wouldn't know, so it still amounts to the same thing. Being held prisoner!'

Connor chuckled, slipping an arm around her again as they followed the dog down through the neat front garden and the warm, still evening air. He was smiling, that slow sensuous smile that even now was doing funny things to Fern's stomach, and, in a voice heavy with innuendo, he said, 'I know. But think what special prize you might have missed if I'd let you get away.'

She gave a tremulous little laugh, wondering if he realised the full potential of his ability to excite her—guessing he would and knowing full well he wasn't talking about the necklace. Not its monetary value, anyway. He had given her riches today far beyond the boundaries of any material wealth, in his lovemaking, in his so openly expressed need of her, in his wonderful proposal of marriage.

'I love you,' she whispered, finding his answering statement, strong and overflowing, in his eyes, feeling it in the lips that brushed her temple and the arm that tightened around her, so that she snuggled against him, knowing that that was the greatest treasure of all.

Let
HARLEQUIN ROMANCE®
take you

BACK TO THE  RANCH

Come to the Diamond B Ranch,
near Fawn Creek, Arizona.

Meet Seth Brody, rancher. And Janna Whitley, city girl.
He's one man who's hard to impress. And she's a woman
with a lot to prove.

Read THE TENDERFOOT by Patricia Knoll,
January's hilarious Back to the Ranch title!

Available wherever Harlequin books are sold.

RANCH8

NEW YORK TIMES Bestselling Author

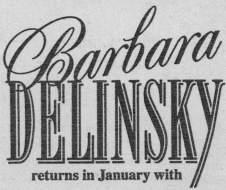

Barbara
DELINSKY

returns in January with

THE REAL THING

Stranded on an island off the coast of Maine,
Deirdre Joyce and Neil Hersey got the
solitude they so desperately craved—
but they also got each other, something they
hadn't expected. Nor had they expected
to be consumed by a desire so powerful
that the idea of living alone again was
unimaginable. A marrige of "convenience"
made sense—or did it?

BOB7

 HARLEQUIN®